STORMY PASSAGE

Three years before, Emma and Ross had gone through a marriage of convenience to allow Emma, who is British, to stay and work in America as Personal Assistant to Ross's father, Thomas. Ross had moved away to Florida, and the plan had been for them to eventually divorce. When Thomas becomes ill, Emma decides to seek out Ross and bring him back to see his father. But there are complications when she realises she is in love with Ross.

Books by Suzanne Clarke
in the Linford Romance Library:

CHANGE OF HEART
SECOND CHANCE
ONCE IN A LIFETIME

1

Emma watched the stunt show from an upper row at the back of the auditorium. She didn't want to be near to the action. She needed to get herself ready for the impending confrontation, which she knew wouldn't be easy.

The stuntmen were acting out Wild West scenes among the two-dimensional buildings of the saloon, jail, hotel and general store erected in the dusty arena. She noticed a clean-shaven man was doing most of the gun-shooting and high dives.

The rest of the audience was enthralled by the raucous show while Emma yawned behind her hand. It had been a very long day. In fact, she'd had little sleep in the last three days since Mr Hamilton's physician had delivered his warning words: Thomas Hamilton had to decrease his workload immediately, and cut out all unnecessary stress unless he wanted to bring on another heart attack.

Thomas had suffered a mild one four years ago and the results from these latest tests hadn't been good. She'd never seen him so depressed and it worried her. Because of this, she was here in Florida on her errand of mercy, one she'd never have undertaken unless it was urgent.

The show continued, amidst loud gunshots and controlled explosions which she disregarded as she stared hard at the chief 'baddie' in black. Already she had sat through two other stunt shows in this film studio's theme park hoping to catch a glimpse of the man she was seeking. Fortunately, after the last one, she'd found someone who knew Ross and told her where he was working today.

At the end of the show, the man acting as the Master of Ceremonies announced the names of the players in turn and the audience applauded.

Finally, he said, 'And as the arch villain — Ross Hamilton!'

The fair streaks of his now visible brown hair gleamed in the brilliant sunshine. As he took his bow he glanced up, and she felt as if his steady gaze had sought out hers in the crowd.

The audience slowly began to filter out through the auditorium's exits. Like the other shows, the stunt players came to the arena's front barriers to chat to the park's visitors as they left.

Purposely taking her time, she let the others in her row go first down the steep steps to ground level before following them, all the while watching to make sure Ross was still there.

Nearing the bottom of the flight, she saw he was chatting to two pretty girls. Typical of him, she mused silently while watching her step. He'd always been popular with the women, which was why she'd been puzzled for the last three years by past events. Ross had helped her so why should she question it?

Because it didn't make sense to her and as she loved an orderly life, it still rankled her. There were questions only Ross could answer and until then she wouldn't be satisfied.

Reaching the ground level, with feet which felt as though they were becoming heavier by the second, she strolled to where he was leaning casually over the barrier. Their eyes met but she found she couldn't utter a word.

'Emma?'

Nodding, she couldn't tear her gaze from his. Until this minute, she'd forgotten how sensual his green eyes were.

'What are you doing here?' he enquired further when she remained silent.

'We have to talk, Ross,' she whispered.

'What is it, Em? What's happened?'

'It's your father.'

She briefly explained the situation, but omitted the fact that it had been her idea to find Ross.

4

His father didn't want him to be bothered.

'Emma, he has a life in Florida,' Thomas had said. 'He made his decision to leave us.'

'Ross should be told the truth so he can make up his mind,' Emma argued.

'Why did I think that's what you'd say?' Thomas said, laughing for the first time in weeks.

'It's probably because of me that Ross left town so it's only fair that I should try to make amends before — '

'Before it's too late?' Thomas shook his head. 'I'll be around for a long time yet if I do as they say. I've got to learn to take things easy and to delegate the responsibility of the company to others.'

'So my father isn't in hospital?' Ross asked, touching her arm gently.

'No. He's at home resting,' she said, slightly breathless from their unexpected physical contact. 'Luckily it was just a scare. But there will be changes in the company and as you're one of the directors we felt you should be told immediately.'

'You've got along fine without me for the past few years — why the sudden concern?'

'Weren't you listening?' she cried. 'Your father has to stop worrying but that won't change while there's this trouble between the two of you. Please, Ross, come back. It really would help — I know it would,' she begged earnestly.

He sighed and stared up at the azure sky for several heart-stopping moments before confronting her again.

'Have you checked into a hotel here?'

She nodded and told him its name.

'I didn't know how long it'd take to find you.'

'Then you haven't booked your return flight?'

'There wasn't much point. I wasn't certain whether you had moved on to California. Your friend mentioned you were going there quite soon.'

'I had an offer,' he drawled, deep in

6

thought. 'Look, I have some things to sort out here. If you catch a cab to the hotel and pack, I'll drive by in an hour and collect you on the way to my apartment.'

'Shall I phone the airport and make our reservations?' she enquired, pleased he was going home after so long.

'No. We'll take my car. If we leave by seven, we'll be home in time for breakfast tomorrow.'

The notion of being in close proximity to him for up to twelve hours took the edge off her recent contented feelings. There were a lot of miles between here and the town of Beaufort which had become her home since she arrived in America three and a half years ago.

'I'll see you in an hour,' she told him. 'I'll be waiting in reception.'

When she arrived at her hotel she asked for her bill to be made up then went upstairs to her room and took a much-needed shower.

Fifteen minutes later, she was ready

to pack and pay the bill.

She only had to wait a few minutes before she saw Ross coming through the glass doors. Out of his earlier cowboy costume, he didn't look very different now in his faded jeans and white short-sleeved shirt, she mused.

'You're ready to go.' It was a comment, not a question. He stooped to grasp her holdall and she hurried after him to keep up with his long strides.

Opening the boot of a red sports coupé, he threw in her bag then turned to her as he slammed it shut.

'Is anyone staying at the house to look after Pop?'

'Your sister Annetta has moved back while I'm away.'

'I thought you had your own place in town.'

She felt the blush rising to her cheeks under his close scrutiny.

'I have. I stayed over for the last few nights. Thomas and I had a lot to discuss, plus I didn't think it was wise to leave him alone.'

The animosity in his gaze was visible.

'I guess not,' he drawled, not sounding wholly convinced as he unlocked the doors.

They drove in silence to his apartment, a journey which only took five minutes. It felt strange to be in his presence after such a long while.

'Come up and wait,' he told her, parking the car in a space below the modern three-storey block.

Following him up a flight of stairs to the first floor, Emma stopped behind him as he took out his keys and opened a door.

When they went inside she was surprised by the sparseness of the decor. Ross came from a wealthy family and she'd expected to see some evidence of it in his new home!

'I only moved into this apartment four months ago,' he explained, leading her into the kitchen. 'Help yourself to a drink from the refrigerator while I change and get my things together.'

Finding a chilled diet cola, she strolled around the large kitchen then the living room as she sipped it directly from the can.

'Hi there!'

Emma turned to see who'd spoken. It was an attractive girl with long, tousled, dark hair. She pulled her short, cotton wrap tighter around her and secured its belt.

'Can I get you a drink?'

Emma held up her can, shocked by the girl's arrival and state of undress.

'Oh, you have one.' The girl yawned. 'You'll have to excuse me — we had a late night celebrating. You know how it is.'

Not really, Emma considered silently. The last thing she wanted to know were the details of the relationship between Ross and this girl.

'And you are?' the girl enquired, coming out of the kitchen door with a small bottle of mineral water in her hand.

'Emma Taylor.'

The brunette seemed perplexed as her brow creased. 'Are you British?'

'I'm from England,' Emma confirmed precisely. 'Near London.'

'I thought so,' the girl said, obviously pleased she'd guessed correctly. 'Are you here on vacation, too?'

'No. I live in South Carolina. I work for Ross's father,' Emma replied, glancing at her watch and wondering how long he'd be.

'He has a real estate business, yeah?'

'That's right.'

Emma had to admit she wasn't too impressed with the girl. She was pretty enough, and young, but she'd expected to find him with someone with a bit more — finesse.

'What work do you do?' the girl asked, as Emma studied a picture on the wall.

'I'm Mr Hamilton's Personal Assistant. For the last two years I've been dealing with a retirement community project.'

'Is it interesting?'

'Yes, it is. I wouldn't have stayed so long otherwise. This project is the first I've worked through from the initial stage.'

The girl nodded thoughtfully.

'It sounds good. I wish I had an occupation like yours.'

'What do you do?' Emma asked.

'OK, Emma, I'm ready to go,' Ross announced, bursting into the lounge with a flourish. 'Hi, honey. I didn't think you were here.'

'Where are you going?' The girl noticed the two holdalls by his feet.

'Home. I'm not sure how long I'll be. My father's ill and I should see him.'

'What about the apartment?'

'I'll call in the week and let you know what's happening.'

'Emma?' The brunette murmured as a thought permeated her drowsy mind. 'Isn't that the name of your wife?'

'Weren't you two introduced?' Ross asked, sliding his arm around the brunette's waist. 'No doubt my liberated wife is still calling herself by her

12

single name.' He chuckled.

'It's a bad habit of mine,' Emma declared apologetically. 'As Ross knows, I use my maiden surname so the other employees don't think I got the job just because of my connections with the family.'

Her full official title — Mrs Roscoe Taylor Hamilton — always sounded to her like the name of a firm of solicitors! And that, together with wanting to cause the least embarrassment at work meant that she preferred plain Emma Taylor as she'd been before they'd stood in front of the judge in his office.

'Maybe I'll still be in Beaufort for our third anniversary,' he pondered aloud. 'It's the tenth of next month, isn't it?'

'I'd go crazy if my husband didn't remember the date of our wedding!' The brunette looked between them in astonishment.

'Our marriage is hardly a conventional one,' Ross replied.

'So you've told me before now but I thought — '

13

'We really should get off, Lindy,' Ross cut in. 'It's gonna be a long night.'

'I hope you have a safe journey. Remember to call.'

'It's nice to have met you, Lindy,' Emma said, moving towards the door.

'Who knows? Maybe we'll meet again, huh?'

While Ross stored his bags in the boot and some other bits on the rear seat, Emma fumed inwardly as she waited by the car for him.

Standing to his full height, he glanced across the roof at her and caught her expression. He raised a puzzled brow.

'Ross, why did you have to tell her?' she demanded in a level tone.

'What? That it's our third anniversary next month?'

'That I'm your wife!' she hissed as he slid into his seat. She got in her side and slammed the door.

'Because you are! Or have you forgotten already?'

'I can hardly forget it,' she grunted.

14

'But it doesn't mean I have to be happy about it!'

The car braked heavily and she was thrown forward into the belt.

'Emma, this will be a darned long drive tonight so let's get things straight! We both know why we got married — to give you a name and the right to stay here legally. We may not like one another but if my father sees us arguing it isn't gonna help his condition any!'

'I'll promise to behave just so long as you do,' she countered.

'Then we understand one another?'

She nodded.

'And you agree to play by my rules? Otherwise I'll drive you to the airport now and you can wait there for a flight. I could quite easily call home to find out how he is.'

'You have to come back!' she pleaded. 'You can't expect to heal the rift over the phone.'

'As you know, my father's an astute man. When he sees us together he's gonna think we're either trying to make

15

another go of our marriage . . . ' His voice trailed off and he continued to regard her reaction. 'Or he'll think we're going to announce our imminent divorce.'

'He knows our marriage didn't work out, Ross. He understood why you left.'

'But I'm sure it hasn't stopped him hoping we'd eventually get back together.'

She had been so hasty in her decision to find Ross to tell him of his father's illness and the company changes that she hadn't stopped for a moment to consider why Thomas had been so delighted. The elderly man was hoping for a reconciliation!

Her widened eyes reflected the alarm and turmoil of emotions she was feeling inside.

'Well, honey,' Ross drawled as he headed out into the stream of traffic, 'are you prepared to put up with a little romancing for his sake or shall we call it a day and I drop you off at the airport?'

Thomas badly needed to see his son,

though he was too proud to admit it. If she returned alone, it could set him back further and could she live with that on her conscience? But the alternative was trying to successfully act as if she loved Ross.

'Well?' he prompted her, slowing the car as they approached a large sign which indicated that the roads to the airport and the one leading to the north were diverging.

Quickly she assessed her options and chose what she thought to be the lesser of the two evils.

'Beaufort.' She sighed with anguish.

2

Luckily Ross turned on the radio so that the silence which was hanging so heavily in the car was broken by a chatty DJ who at least gave Emma something to listen to.

Ross turned down the volume when an advertisement for a local restaurant began.

'So what's been happening in my absence? Has he promoted you on to the board yet?' he enquired suddenly in an icy tone.

'No. You know he'll only have his immediate family on it.'

'I thought he'd have made an exception for you, Em.'

'I'm his Personal Assistant now, nothing more.'

'And what have you been doing as his Personal Assistant?'

She went over the details of the

retirement community and another which was at the planning stage.

'Who's stepped in to take over his work?'

'Temporarily, it's been split between myself and Marshall Delacroix.'

'I don't think I know him. Is he any good?'

Emma shivered.

'He works very hard and is loyal to the firm. Thomas is pleased with him.'

She didn't add that Marshall was also pleasant to be with outside of office hours; they'd recently had several meals together out of town, though it wasn't common knowledge amongst their colleagues.

'How do you think he'd feel if another Hamilton was to take over at the helm?'

'You?' she asked in a horrified whisper.

'My brother Bill wouldn't be interested in leaving that law practice in Manhattan,' he said, momentarily glancing across at her. 'Not when he's studied for years to get where he is. Annetta has her family to care for, so I guess that leaves only myself.'

'Don't you have a contract with that theme park?'

Ross chuckled as he overtook a slower car.

'Why do I get the impression you're perfectly happy for me to make a flying visit but not to settle permanently in Beaufort?'

'I didn't mean it to sound like that. It's come as a surprise that you're considering returning to the family business, that's all,' she explained.

'My contract finished a month ago but I didn't want to renew it until I really decided what my next move is going to be. I haven't decided yet.'

'I thought you wanted to get back into films. You said that you enjoyed the years you spent in California and going around the world,' she challenged.

Music had returned onto the radio station but he leaned forward and switched it off.

'People change.' He sighed wistfully. 'I feel it's time to put down some roots of my own — whether it's in California or Beaufort.'

She gazed over at him in amazement. Outwardly he mightn't have changed but this didn't sound like the Ross Hamilton she'd known.

'Your father would be pleased if you chose the latter.'

'But how would you feel, Emma, having your husband living in the same town?'

'Soon your father will be stronger and we'll be able to explain things to him.'

'It'd be easier all round if I did head west. We could get a quiet divorce,' he mused aloud, briefly gazing at her. 'You've got your papers so it's not as if you're here illegally.'

Theirs had been a marriage of convenience yet it didn't stop her hating the idea of getting divorced.

'We'd better fill up on gas and I could do with a coffee,' Ross said, flicking the indicator switch.

Leaving the highway, they drove to a nearby petrol station. While he filled the car, Emma went into the shop and poured coffee from a percolator on the side into two polystyrene mugs. Having added cream and sugar to hers, she thought back to how Ross took his.

'As you like it,' she declared handing him the steaming mug after stirring it. 'Black with one sugar.'

'You remembered.' Ross looked slightly amazed.

'How could I forget? It was worse than cramming for school exams.'

He leaned back against the counter, stretching his body.

'For two people who've never spent the night together in the same bed, we sure know a lot about each other's likes, pet hates, hopes and dreams.'

'Those which we chose to share, you mean,' she parried.

It had been hard for Emma to lie about herself and more than once she had wanted to run back to England.

She'd voiced her worries to Ross and he'd been a wonderful listener. As he knew the reason why his father had initially invited her to live with them, Ross managed to convince her to stay.

Gently and very tactfully, he'd reminded her Thomas had been a good friend to her late father and that she had no immediate family back in England. When her father had died unexpectedly, Thomas, also a widower, had been on the first plane to console her and to stand by her when she made the necessary arrangements.

She owed Thomas a great deal and she'd hoped she could repay part of this debt by finally bringing the two Hamilton men together.

'Would you mind taking over at the wheel for a spell?' Ross asked, draining his mug and throwing it in the bin.

'If you think you can trust me. I think I scared you the first time you took me out in an automatic car,' she recalled, smiling at him.

'I've taken hundred foot drops that

were less terrifying!' he joked.

'Don't worry, though — it's a straightforward road.' Ross stifled a yawn and stretched his muscular arms. 'I need an hour's sleep. I had a late night then I had to be at the park early today.'

She didn't comment that Lindy had informed her of their celebration, though she wondered what it had been for.

'Do you mind if I put the radio back on? This straight road is so boring.'

'Go ahead — you won't be disturbing me,' Ross murmured, his voice already sleepy as he settled down into his seat. 'Wake me in an hour and we'll change over.'

While he slept, she concentrated on the road, keeping faithfully to the speed limit which was sixty-five for most areas. Although Ross had been asleep for an hour, she continued driving, deciding it was preferable to spend as little time awake together as possible.

Eventually she needed to find a

service station to use the bathroom. When she stopped in the forecourt, Ross stirred.

'I won't be a moment,' she told him before heading towards the garage store.

When she returned, Ross was standing in front of the car, stretching his cramped limbs.

'Why didn't you wake me?'

'You looked so peaceful,' she replied, handing him a can of cola. 'I didn't like to disturb you.'

'We'd better get on,' he remarked, looking at his watch then opening the car doors.

She was already tired when she'd arrived in Orlando that day and with concentrating on driving, she found her eyelids becoming heavier as the car devoured the miles. Cuddling into the comfortable, padded seat in the darkness, she fell asleep . . .

★　★　★

When it came, her dream was vivid and even as she slept it shocked her. She dreamed of Ross and how incredibly handsome he was. How deep down she knew she was attracted to him. But theirs was a marriage of convenience and they could never live together as man and wife. Even though she'd often thought about it she knew that it could never work — unless . . .

Someone was touching her now and the dream took a strange turn.

'No, Ross, you're wrong,' she mumbled, confused.

'Hey, what's up?' Ross enquired and his voice was nearer her now. His caress wasn't gentle, he was shaking her. 'Emma?'

'What?' It was pitch-black around her. The sun had gone.

'Emma, wake up. You've been having a bad dream, honey.'

In the darkness she heard a movement and a small light came on.

'Are you OK? You were calling out,' Ross told her, swivelling in his seat to face her.

'Where are we?' There was gloom all around them and she caught her dimly-lit reflection in her window. She looked terrible!

'We're still in Georgia. I pulled over to the side when you cried out. It must have been some nightmare,' he said as he switched off the light and carefully rejoined the road. 'I'll find a place to stop for an hour. I think we both need a break from this.'

She closed her eyes and shivered. That episode was just the prelude to the months of emotional turmoil ahead. No, her living nightmare didn't truly start until a lot later!

3

There were a few other people in the all-night diner which Ross found at the next exit. Sitting at the table and looking around, she guessed from their banter and attire that they were long-distance lorry drivers. The elderly waitress came and took their order, with Emma declining any food.

'Is coffee enough for you?' Ross enquired, relaxing back in his chair.

'Definitely. How could you eat a burger this time of night — or should I say morning?' she retorted, grimacing.

'I need something to keep me going. I haven't eaten since this morning. I was supposed to be going out for dinner with a friend.'

'I'm sorry if I messed up your plans,' she said, then wishing she hadn't sounded so sarcastic. She couldn't seem to help it with Ross around.

'These things happen. There'll be other nights.' He shrugged, emptying a packet of sugar into his black coffee.

'I was shocked when you appeared in the audience. You've changed a lot since I last saw you,' he declared, stirring his drink.

'In what way?' Outwardly, she didn't think she looked that different. A few early nights would get rid of the heavy bags under her eyes.

'You're still a very good-looking woman,' he said, levelling with her frosty stare. 'And there was something else — a naïveté I thought was rather charming.'

'You forget — I've been an old married woman for nearly three years,' she countered, trying to make a joke of it but not succeeding.

'Honey, you were never this cynical before.'

'Maybe it's because I'd never had to live a lie twenty-four hours a day. I can't afford to be open with people in case I say or do the wrong thing.' She longed to add that she had more guts than he had. She'd stayed and put up with all the whispers and pitying glances. 'From the start I should have realised what I was getting myself into. I only have myself to blame.'

'So you've been calling yourself Taylor?' He thanked the waitress as she brought his burger and chips. Ross glanced down at her hand resting on the table top. 'When did you stop wearing the ring?'

'A few months after you went. I thought for a while I should give the impression that I was hoping you'd come back.' Her thoughts strayed to that last awful day but she deliberately put them aside. She couldn't dwell on the past. Not now, with Ross here with her.

'There aren't many people at the company who realise Thomas is my father-in-law,' she added. 'Most of those who are in key positions have only joined in the last few years.'

'Then they're going to be surprised

when they see you wearing a wedding band. You do still have it?'

'It's in my jewellery box at home.' She thought for a few moments as he tucked into his food. 'Do I have to wear it, Ross?'

'If we're making another go of our marriage, it'd look real strange if you didn't. That reminds me,' he said, wiping his mouth with the paper serviette. 'What are our living arrangements going to be? Do you have space at your apartment or shall we move into my father's place until we find somewhere else?'

'No, Ross. Your family knows we haven't been in contact. They'll think it's odd if we suddenly start living together.'

'That's their problem, not ours. Come on, we could really get them talking again.'

'I don't think that's such a great idea.' Emma shook her head disapprovingly.

'Why not?' Ross laughed. 'I've never

31

been one to conform — you know that.'

She certainly did. Ross could have joined his father's company immediately after finishing his business studies but opted instead to head westward and take up the unlikely occupation of stuntman.

Through their period of intense studying, in case the immigration staff tried to trick them, Ross never informed her of why he had turned his back on Hollywood and she always felt it to be their weak link.

Now she was just plain curious, seeing as she knew most of the other details about his habits and earlier life.

'Please, don't do anything wild to upset your father,' she warned him. Suppressing a smile, she added, 'At least not in the first few hours until he's had time to adjust to your presence.'

'You know me so well, honey, it frightens me,' he joked, pushing away his empty plate.

'You're wrong. I may know the facts and figures on your life so I could fill out your cv if I was asked, but I know nothing about what you feel up here,' she said indicating her own forehead.

He raised a questioning brow. 'We lived together at my father's for six months. You must have learned something.'

Picking up her coffee, she leaned back in her chair and cupped the mug in her hands. 'Not a lot. You tend to play things close to your chest.'

'And you don't?' he retaliated, no humour now in his voice.

'Can I top up your coffee?' the waitress's voice cut in from beside them. For the early hours, she was surprisingly cheerful.

'No, but thank you for asking,' Emma answered politely. 'Do you have a rest room? I'd like to rinse my face.'

'Just through there,' the waitress informed her, indicating to a door on the far wall.

* * *

On returning to the restaurant, Emma was startled to find their table was empty. Ross was nowhere to be seen! Rushing to the door, she was alarmed to find his car had gone. With her heart beating wildly, she hurried over to the waitress who was just clearing away their dirty crockery.

'The man I was with — where did he go?' she cried. It was obviously his way of teaching her a lesson — leaving her alone in the back of beyond!

'Don't worry, don't worry.' The waitress hurried up to Emma. 'He's just gone down the road for gas. You come with me. You look as if you could do with some cold juice to perk you up.'

Emma smiled as she saw Ross walk through the door ten minutes later. She thanked the waitress and paid her before striding over to where Ross waited.

'What on earth were you playing at?' she hissed, feeling both irritated by his actions and relieved that he'd come back. 'Do you want me to drive for a while?'

'Admit it, Emma — you're exhausted.' He pulled her around so she confronted him in the light from the diner. 'You look as if you haven't slept for a week. Are you sure you're all right?'

'Please, Ross, let's discuss it later. I'm not up to it right now.'

'Are you holding something back from me about Thomas?'

'No. I told you the truth earlier.' She raked her fingers through her hair, a sign she was nervous or tired — and she was both. 'Please, can't this wait?'

'Tell me now and you might rest easier,' he coaxed her, his hand stroking her arm.

'Thomas didn't tell me but I think I might know what's been causing his recent stress.' She sighed.

'Let's sit in the car,' he suggested as the engine of one of the nearby lorries was started up.

'OK, Emma. What's been going on?'

Ross said when they were settled inside. He turned to face her with his arm resting across the back of her seat.

'Well,' Emma began, 'after he had been to see his doctor, Thomas asked me to come over to the house. He told me he would need plenty of rest, as I've told you. He said there were some letters to be sent off urgently that evening and asked me to go back to sign them for him and then post them.'

'And?' Ross shuffled in his seat impatiently.

'When I got to his office, his ledger was on his desk. You know how he hates computers.' Ross nodded knowingly and she went on. 'I thought I'd help him out by balancing the figures because he hadn't done it for a few days. He'd been very busy.

'When everyone had gone home, I printed off the details from the computer and took them back to my room at his house with his ledger to make sure my calculations were correct. I sat up most of the night trying to get them to tally and the next day, I double-checked all the entries — those on the computer and in the ledger.'

'Maybe Pop was distracted and had got his set of figures wrong.'

'Have you ever known your father not to be meticulous in his paperwork?' she retaliated. 'He even countersigns every payment docket that passes through the office.'

She sighed.

'There were some sheets of paper — I found them under one of his files when I was tidying his desk. He'd been working out some sums in rough, as he doesn't trust calculators either. I'm almost positive he'd been double-checking those same amounts.'

'Have you kept them?'

From his tone, she knew he was trying to hide his anger.

'Of course I have. I was worried about leaving them and the ledger lying around for anyone to read.'

'Are they in the office safe?'

'No. I thought that if someone has

been embezzling company money, they might have access to the safe as well. I put them in my safety deposit box in the bank. I didn't know what else to do — I didn't dare to confront your father, not when the doctor's said he has to avoid stress.'

'You did the right thing. Have you any idea who it could be?'

'None. I've tried to comfort your father — to pretend everything is running smoothly, but it hasn't been easy.'

'You don't have to worry, Emma.' He patted her arm. 'We'll soon find out who did it. They can't have covered their tracks that well.'

Exhaustion and her swirling mass of confused emotions were taking their toll and tears pricked at the corners of her eyes. She couldn't tell him she already knew exactly where the trail led to. The person had covered themselves by implicating her and she now had the ledger in her possession!

Given time, Ross might be convinced of her innocence but at present, in his state of anger, he'd jump to the wrong conclusion.

She shivered with fear thinking of the confrontation which had to happen soon. Although he had an easy-going nature, Ross had a terrible temper when riled, as she'd found out to her cost.

He started up the engine then looked across at her.

'Why didn't you tell me any of this earlier? I could have got our accountants on to it immediately.'

'Even if they were prepared to work at the weekend, they still couldn't do anything until Monday. The paperwork is locked in my deposit box and no-one else has a key, even if the bank had been open.'

'Try to sleep, Em,' he told her as they finally pulled out of the carpark.

* * *

On waking, she was surprised to find dawn was breaking. Her sleep had been deep and thankfully dreamless.

'Shall I take over?' she asked huskily, stretching as much as she could in the limited space. She noted they'd left the highway and were driving down a narrower road.

'There's no need,' he said, glancing across at her for a second. 'We should be there in twenty minutes.'

Her eyebrows rose. 'Have I slept that long? Why didn't you wake me?'

'Didn't I say something similar earlier on during this marathon journey?' he retorted, smiling.

'When we arrive, would you like to come to my apartment for breakfast?' she suggested, hoping to score a few points in her favour. 'Your father doesn't know we're coming back this morning.'

'Illness or not, he'll still be awake early.' Briefly, Ross's eyes flickered in her direction. 'And breakfast will be on the table at six-thirty.'

He was silent for some minutes and he seemed to be weighing up the situation.

'I guess you're right. Although I want to see how he is, it's probably better if we meet him when he's had time to wake up properly. I could do with a shower, but we'll have breakfast at Pop's house.'

The town was so peaceful as they drove through the streets shaded by oaks veiled with grey Spanish moss. Across the stretch of water, the early-morning mist was shrouding the distant islands.

'It's the second house along here,' she informed Ross as they turned into her street. It wasn't grand like his father's but it suited Emma's needs.

When he parked, Ross got out all of her luggage and one of his holdalls.

'Lead the way,' he said, closing the boot quietly.

Carefully she opened the front door she shared with her friendly neighbours. Creeping up the stairs, she felt like a naughty schoolgirl coming home late, though really there was no need, she thought reaching the top of the flight. They'd never complained about her behaviour before and she didn't want to give them reason to now.

'The bathroom is through there,' she said when Ross entered her lounge. 'I'll just get you some clean towels and a new bar of soap.'

Deliberately keeping herself busy so she wouldn't dwell on her problems, she had a pot of coffee brewed by the time she heard Ross turn off the shower. Putting some bread in the toaster, she then set the dining table when she heard the door open. Taking a deep breath to steady herself, she glanced casually over her shoulder. Her eyes widened in alarm.

'There's coffee and toast on the table,' she mumbled, not really knowing where to look when Ross walked in wrapped only in a towel.

The moment was far too intimate for her and she'd forgotten how Ross looked. You could tell he was a sportsman and obviously took great care of his body — more so than Emma remembered.

'I hope you don't mind me sitting down to breakfast dressed like this — it's too warm to get changed.' He laughed as he noticed Emma's surprised look.

'You should have opened the window like I do,' she remarked pouring out the coffee and passing him a mug.

'I didn't like to make too much noise in case it woke your neighbours,' he growled, spooning sugar into his drink. 'Don't worry, I'll be out of here as soon as I can.'

From the finality in his voice, she felt he wasn't just talking about her flat but her life, too!

4

Although she could have used tiredness as a plausible excuse to remain in her flat, Emma didn't want to miss the reconciliation between father and son. She felt to blame and wanted to be there to see Thomas's delighted expression.

Having had a shower and changed into a cool, cotton dress, she felt less exhausted but guessed it was adrenaline that was keeping her going.

'Do you know what to do?' Ross asked her, turning in his seat when he had stopped his car on Thomas's wide driveway.

Glancing up at the imposing, pillared mansion, she felt the nerves flutter in her stomach. She felt more nervous than she had when they're returned from marrying in secret.

'We've been through it twice already,'

she replied, looking at him. Thankfully he was fully clothed again — in a clean pair of jeans and fresh T-shirt. 'I know the drill.'

'Just wanted to make sure,' he grumbled, opening his door but looking at her when she remained in her seat. 'Something wrong?'

She took a deep breath.

'I'll be OK,' she murmured, stifling a yawn.

'I'll run you back shortly. I want you up early in the morning so we can be at the bank when it opens.'

The nerves were getting worse and her stomach lurched nauseously. She let him lead her by the hand to the huge front door which was open when they arrived. One of his father's staff was standing beside it.

'Welcome back, sir, ma'am.' The elderly man who acted as butler and chauffeur bowed his head with reverence. 'Mr Hamilton is in the parlour.'

'Thanks, Charles. Could you bring

my bags in, please? The car's unlocked.'

'Certainly, sir. I'll take them up to your old room,' he answered, glancing between Ross and Emma. She could tell what he was thinking but she knew he wouldn't dare ask any questions, waiting instead until he heard the gossip.

Ross's fingers grasped her hand tighter when Charles left them.

'Do we have to?' she pleaded, glancing down at their entwined fingers.

'Yes, we have to! Come on.'

He tapped lightly on the open parlour door.

'What is it, Charles?' she heard Thomas call out.

Tugging Emma into the room behind him, Ross said, 'It's me, Pop.'

Thomas turned in his armchair and the newspaper dropped from his hands on to his lap.

'So she found you, son.' Emma could hear the relief in his voice.

'Yes sir,' Ross remarked, turning her

46

around so they were standing side by side.

'I didn't expect you to return so soon, Emma,' he said, smiling at her and getting up slowly from his chair. 'Did you get the morning flight?'

'We drove up in my car,' Ross replied as his father approached him.

Glancing around, she saw from his expression he was visibly shocked by his father's appearance. Thomas's face still looked pale and drawn, though he was better than he had been.

'Son?' Thomas held out his hand. It was trembling.

Dropping Emma's hand, Ross stepped forward to throw his arms around his father and hugged him. Tears stung Emma's eyes as relief surged through her body. She turned away. There had been few shows of open affection between the two men and she didn't want to make them feel embarrassed.

A movement beside her signalled the moment was over. Lightly, Ross took her hand again in his.

'How long are you planning on staying, son?' Thomas stood over them.

'That depends,' Ross drawled, his fingers closing over hers as he gazed at her.

'Have you two had breakfast?'

Ross was a marvellous actor, she thought, noting the twinkle of pleasure in his father's eyes.

'Not yet. Are you hungry now, honey?' he enquired in such a smooth tone she wanted to kick him! He thought he could get round her so easily!

'I'll find Charles and get him to organise it.' Thomas smiled and left the room.

'You couldn't be more blatant if you tried!' she hissed quietly. 'He's bound to think everything's just perfect between us now.'

'What's wrong with that?' He chuckled.

'We're supposed to be going slowly though! You promised me, Ross.'

48

She tried to pull herself away from his embrace but his hold tightened as he turned her to confront him directly. Without warning, he bent his head and kissed her on the lips. She mumbled her discontent through her closed mouth and tried to escape.

His hand was stroking her back as his continued kisses coaxed her to respond. Her pulse accelerated while the rest of her body suddenly felt alive again.

She heard a rustle in the room and she pulled away, blushing when she saw Thomas had returned.

'I'm sorry.' He, too, seemed embarrassed and went to leave.

'We should be the ones who are sorry, Pop,' Ross called to him, letting his arm remain across her back.

Thomas sat in his armchair and looked at them with a serious expression. 'I'm not interfering in your lives. You're old enough to make your own decisions, whatever they may be. I was lucky to have a good marriage — I still miss your Momma, even though she's been gone these ten years. But you have to realise it doesn't just happen — you have to work at it, son.'

'I know, Pop.'

'Do you?' Thomas countered. 'We had some bad times along the way and I could have quite easily walked out on your Momma. I didn't. I stayed and between us, we worked it out.'

Thomas relaxed back into his cushions.

'Real love grows from respect but you have to give it time. You rushed into marriage while the initial flames of desire burned. Like a fire, you have to rekindle it from time to time else it goes out like a damp squib!'

Ross laughed at his father's description and drew her to his firm embrace.

'You're right — it's time we need. We're still very attracted to one another. That was obvious when we met up yesterday. We've been talking most of the night and although we both want to give it another shot, we'd prefer to keep our relationship quiet for the time being.'

'I understand, son. Will you be moving back into the house, Emma?'

She tried to moisten her dry throat.

'I'm not sure. I haven't had time to think yet — I don't expect things to turn around in just one day!'

'We'll have to see how we work together, too,' Ross informed him.

'You're quitting your job?'

Ross explained the details in full.

'If you want me at Hamiltons, that is.'

'Of course I do, son. I couldn't be more pleased although Emma has stepped in marvellously for me.'

'I could do with a bit less responsibility,' she declared honestly.

'And I'm sure Marshall will understand. Tomorrow he and Emma can tell you what's going on. If you need to know anything, you can always ask me.'

Thomas nodded to Charles when he indicated their breakfast was ready.

'The doctor said you were to rest and that's what you're going to do. Emma will give me all the help I need, isn't that right, honey?'

'Just don't let working together jeopardise your relationship,' Thomas warned them, standing up.

'Oh, we won't.' Ross smiled as he took her hand and helped her to her feet.

'I'd like to ask you both a favour,' Emma cut in. 'Would you mind if I continued to be called Taylor — at least for a short while?'

'People are going to talk in town,' Ross said, sliding his arm around her waist. 'Although I suppose none of them know whether we actually got divorced when we separated.'

'If anyone at the company asks me directly then I'll tell them the truth that I prefer to go by my single name at work.' Marshall would have a big shock and she knew she should tell him before he heard it through the office grapevine. 'Would you mind if I skipped breakfast? I'm feeling very tired.'

'I'll run you home. It'll only take a

few minutes,' Ross said strolling beside her to the parlour door.

'It's OK, I'll walk. I really need some fresh air — I have a headache starting,' she told them, rubbing her temple with her fingertips to give credence to her excuse.

'Will you be coming for dinner tonight?' Thomas asked. 'I'd like to ask Annetta's family over.'

'You should be resting,' she chided him gently as she said her goodbyes.

'It'll be wonderful to have my family here together again. It's a shame Bill's missing this,' Thomas said before strolling off towards the dining room.

'Shall I call for you at seven?' Ross prompted, not giving her a choice in the matter.

★   ★   ★

Walking home, she was furious with Ross — for making her pretend they were trying to reconcile a relationship which hadn't got off the ground, for

53

kissing her and for making her remember what she'd been missing for two and a half years!

She was not going to let herself fall in love with him all over again! She wiped away a tear which trickled down her cheek and strode faster down the sleepy street to her home.

Although her body needed sleep she was much too angry as she lay in her bed, the curtains blacking out the brilliant, late May morning sky. Beneath the cotton sheet, she turned over and huffed in annoyance. How dare Ross come back into her life and turn it upside down the way he had!

Getting up, she went to the refrigerator and poured herself a glass of milk, hoping it would help sleep to come. Remember what Ross can be like, she warned herself, sliding under the sheet again.

But instead of recalling those bad moments in their relationship, all that came to mind were the hours of laughter and growing friendship which led her to fall in love with him, though she'd been stupid to believe Ross felt anything close to love for her.

He'd made his decision and used his Hollywood acting experience to make everyone, including Emma, believe he was madly in love. After four months of marriage, being constantly 'on view,' it took its toll on both of them.

Suddenly Ross withdrew any public display of affection and it hurt her badly. She loved him and lived for his embraces. During the last two months he had spent more and more time away from the house.

When she'd eventually summoned up the courage to confront him, he didn't deny he'd been seeing another woman.

She couldn't really understand why he was doing it. Did he really care so little about her that he thought it was perfectly acceptable to flaunt his lady friends right under her nose. He didn't even seem to care that he'd upset her

— just carried on as normal.

It was then that a huge row ensued which ended with Ross walking out of the suite he shared with Emma in Thomas's house.

She'd pleaded with him not to go — what if people found out that theirs had been a marriage of convenience — she could well be thrown out of the States. But more importantly, she didn't want him to leave because she knew she'd fallen deeply in love with him.

Getting up from her bed, she went over to her dressing-table to comb her hair and found Ross had left his aftershave behind when he'd used her room to dress that morning.

Removing the cap, she sniffed it and its sensual musky aroma had her remembering how good it felt to be held in his arms and to be kissed by him.

It was as if he'd never been away and they'd never had those last arguments. Father and son were reunited, seeming to be as close as they ever were. But would she and Ross have a reconciliation or would things become so bad she'd be the one leaving Beaufort this time?

5

Her doorbell sounded at a quarter to seven and, glancing out of her window, Emma noticed no car was parked outside. Hurrying down the stairs, she prayed Marshall hadn't dropped by as he'd done a few times in the past month, not when Ross was due to arrive!

'You're early,' she remarked on seeing Ross standing there. 'Do you want to come up and wait while I finish getting ready?'

He looked very different from that morning. Recently showered, his hair was groomed though still slightly damp. Dressed in elegant pale grey slacks and a white shirt, open at the collar, his suit jacket was thrown over his shoulder.

'Sure,' he replied, closing the door after him and following her up to her flat.

'I won't be a minute,' she informed him.

'You look lovely tonight, Emma,' he drawled, smiling as he cast his eyes over her turquoise cotton dress which she'd chosen after a lot of deliberation.

'Can I get you a drink? I think I have a bottle of the bourbon that you like in the cupboard.' She regarded him as he strolled around her living room.

'That'd be good,' he answered, stopping to admire one of her framed pictures.

'Did you decorate this place yourself?' he enquired, taking the tumbler she was holding out to him.

She nodded as he sipped it.

'I should have guessed when I came here this morning. I was too tired to appreciate it then. You've always had a good eye for colour.'

When she'd taken on the top apartment, she'd asked the landlords for permission to change from the rose-strewn wallpaper to something less taxing on the eyes. Now the hues throughout the rooms were like those of a glorious Southern sunset: cream and peach with hints of deep orange.

Ross sat in an armchair and smoothed the material of his trouser leg as he crossed one over the other. He pointed to a framed watercolour on the wall. It was of a local scene — shrimp boats in the misty harbour at dawn. 'Is that one of yours?' he asked.

Again she nodded. 'I did it about a year ago.'

'It's very good. I saw the one you did of the house today. Pop has it in pride of place in the dining room where it deserves to be.'

She blushed. 'I gave it to him on his last birthday. It only took me a weekend to do it.'

He relaxed back in the deep peach scatter cushions.

'It would take others months to get it right. You should try and get your work into one of the local galleries. I'm certain you'd have no problem being accepted.'

'I don't have much spare time these days for my hobby. I doodle when I'm on the phone and that's about it!'

Leaning forward, he got his glass and took a long sip.

'I remember when I had to learn about your past — you said you turned down an art course in favour of a secretarial one. I think you made the wrong decision.'

'I didn't have a lot of choice at the time.' She sighed wistfully. 'I was sixteen, my dad was a widower who owned an ailing business. At least with secretarial training I knew I had a better chance of getting a permanent job at the end, as there aren't so many openings for artists.'

'So you sacrificed your dreams for loyalty?'

'You make it sound as though dad made me give it up. You couldn't be further from the truth. He was really upset. I decided to follow what I considered was the correct career path.'

'No regrets?' he asked, cupping the

tumbler in his large hands.

'None.' Her chin tilted proudly. 'I got a good wage so I was able to pay the bills when he sold the business until he found a new job.'

'I meant personally speaking. You seem to have to sacrifice any dreams you may have for other people.'

From the tone of his voice she knew he was now talking about her loyalty to Thomas.

'I've been very happy here in America. I have a job which I enjoy tremendously. I have a good boss who is a great friend, too. Why should I have any regrets? I'm a lot better off than most people I know — and I'm not just talking about my financial situation.'

'But you'd be much happier if you didn't have this cloud of marriage hanging over you?' he suggested, reading her expression correctly.

'Wouldn't you?' she countered. 'I've learned to live with it — eventually.'

He chuckled deeply.

'Three years next month — where

has the time gone?' His eyes suddenly lost their twinkle. 'When I saw you in that audience, Em, I immediately thought you'd come to ask for a divorce.'

'It's no wonder I thought you were relieved!' she jested. 'I'm sorry I didn't give you the news you wanted to hear.'

He looked at his watch.

'Did you say you had things still to do?' he enquired in a clipped voice. 'Pop has asked Annetta and her family over. We should get back.'

Going to her bedroom, Emma put a coat of lipstick on her lips and regarded herself critically in the full-length mirror on the back of her door. She had lost a few pounds in his absence so her figure was now svelte without looking emaciated.

Although she'd eventually fallen asleep that afternoon for four hours, she knew it'd take at least a week to regain her full strength. Yet it wouldn't be an easy task with Ross in her waking and sleeping thoughts!

Picking up a light jacket, she re-entered the living room and Ross stood to greet her.

'This is for you,' he said, taking a small maroon velvet case from his jacket's inside pocket.

Her brow creased in puzzlement.

'You were meant to have this that Christmas,' he informed her when he handed her the gift. 'I found it today in my closet. Better late than never.'

Emma opened the lid and was astonished to find a beautiful, gold necklace lying on the cream satin. 'It's lovely,' she stammered, 'but I can't take it.'

'Why ever not?'

'It's so . . . ' She stared down at it. It must have cost him a fortune! The initials of E and H were entwined in old-fashioned script on a pendant and set in diamonds. It was dainty and very elegant.

'There's only one woman I know with those initials and I'll be bound if

I'm going out to find another!' His fingers took it from the satin. 'Let's not argue. I'd say you deserve it.'

Moving behind her, he put the gold piece around her neck. His warm fingers momentarily brushed her neck as he did up the clasp and she shivered inside. Glancing down to see the diamonds sparkling against her skin, she smiled with pleasure.

'If you're really sure,' she offered and he caught her shoulders and pivoted her around to face him. 'Thank you, Ross.' Standing on tiptoes, she kissed his smooth cheek.

'Did you have a bad time when I left?'

'Not really. Most people were too polite to ask what had happened.' She licked her lips nervously and she could taste the light fragrance of his aftershave on them. 'Oh, I've just remembered.' Rushing to her bedroom, glad to have an excuse to leave his touch, she returned with his bottle. 'You left this here today.'

He put it in his pocket and regarded her seriously.

'It wasn't meant to happen that way, honey.'

'We both know it couldn't have gone on for ever the way it was. We were silly to think we could manage to lead a normal life in abnormal circumstances.'

'You've grown up a lot since then. Maybe we both have,' he added pensively. 'As soon as Pop is stronger, we'll tell him it's not working and we're separating for good.

'You have my word — there'll be no animosity on my part and I'll make sure you'll still be welcome at the house whether I'm there or not.' His eyebrows lifted. 'You don't mind waiting a while though?'

'How can I refuse?' she remarked, gazing down with admiration at his present, her fingers toying with the pendant. She raised her eyes to meet his. 'You gave up your status as a bachelor for me.'

'Shall we go?' He cut into her

thoughts but just then her phone rang.

'It's probably Thomas wondering where we are.' She laughed and went striding over to the phone on the far table. 'Hello?'

She stiffened as she heard Marshall's drawl on the other end.

'Hi, Emma. I was trying to get hold of you yesterday.'

'I had to go out of town,' she replied with caution and glancing over at Ross who was standing by her door.

'I got those concert tickets you said you wanted.' He didn't sound happy. 'They were for last night.'

'I'm sorry — I completely forgot about it. I had some personal things to attend to.' She turned, her back towards Ross. 'I'll pay you back for the tickets. Look, I can't talk now — it's very difficult. I'm just going out,' she whispered into the mouthpiece.

'Shall I come around later?'

'No!' she hissed then lowered her voice again. 'We'll have lunch tomorrow. I'll explain then.'

'You can tell me in the office,' he replied, sounding less offended now. 'Then we can look forward to having lunch together.'

'OK — I'll see you tomorrow,' she murmured.

She took a deep breath before turning back to Ross again.

'It was a friend who was worried where I'd got to,' she informed Ross, wishing she could have sounded more convincing and that she hadn't blushed quite so deeply.

'I didn't expect you to lead a nun's life, Emma,' he remarked as she passed him.

'He's only a friend,' she insisted, locking the door to her flat. 'And we've only had a few meals — nothing more.'

'You don't have to explain to me, honey.'

Facing him in the hallway, she knew she didn't but it helped to salvage her conscience. It wasn't as if Ross would feel jealous — he was living with Lindy in Orlando. Once the end of their marriage was announced, would she be coming here to join him? She couldn't bear to ask him — not yet.

★   ★   ★

'Do you want me to go straight to the bank in the morning and bring the stuff back to you at the office?' she enquired when they were strolling down a residential street, the Episcopal Church of St Helena directly ahead of them.

'We may as well go there together. I can take them on to the accountant afterwards.'

'Won't you go over them first?' she persisted. 'I'd like to point out where the problems are.' It might help if he thought she wasn't holding anything back.

'We'll see.' Chuckling suddenly, he caught her arm and led her into the entrance of the walled graveyard. 'I haven't been through here for years.'

A cold shiver trailed down her back as he propelled her down the narrow path alongside the spired church between the old stones, his arm around her waist. 'We used to come here after trick or treating,' he told her. 'Being the eldest, Billy tried to scare us.'

She gave a start when a crow cawed loudly in a tree near them.

'Poor Annetta ran home crying and Pop warned him never to do it again.'

He pulled her to a stop by a family plot that had a low, iron railing running around it.

'But you, of course, were very brave, even though you were the youngest,' she said, looking around at him and noticed he was staring at the largest stone which was slightly askew.

'I could only have been about six then,' he replied, still reading the faint inscription. 'Billy said the spirit of the old man haunted our family on All Hallows Eve. That was the night he drowned when his boat and his crew went down in a bad storm off the coast.'

She could read the name on the now mostly moss-covered stone: *William Roscoe Hamilton*. Underneath she deciphered the words: *Sea captain of Plymouth, England and South Carolina*.

'Your forefathers were English, too,' she mused aloud.

'This William was. He was an old rogue.' His smile broadened when she looked at him. 'Sea captain is a euphemistic term for what he really did.'

'What did he do?' she asked, intrigued to know a bit about Ross's history.

He caught her arm and led her down the path.

'Apparently he left England to escape a prison sentence. Although he came to the colony to start a new life with his family as a fisherman, he found it easier to revert to his old ways. Many Spanish and English ships were in this area in those days and a lot were plundered out at sea.'

'You're saying he was a pirate?' she challenged.

'We're not sure if he took part in any of that, but he supposedly made a good living from running illicit goods along the coast.'

'So why does he haunt your family every Hallowe'en?' she enquired, totally disbelieving his story.

'He's supposed to come looking for his gold that he stashed away for his wife and children.'

'It's a good story.' Emma nodded her head, smiling.

'You have to admit that his stone is crooked, Emma.'

'If I was the same age as Annetta was then on that night, maybe I'd believe your brother's unlikely yarn. But that's all it is — a tall story!'

'Really? Some years ago, part of the grounds of my father's house had to be dug up, for new sewerage pipes to be installed. That part of the site, which has been in our family since they settled here, had been a formal garden.

'You've probably seen the old prints of it — it was the pride of the Hamiltons and Pop hated to see it decimated by diggers.'

'Yes, I've seen them. Go on,' she prompted him in his implausible tale that Thomas had never mentioned during his long reminiscences.

'They found a small chest. It's padlock was rusted but it was still secure. The foreman brought it to my father who got the man to find a crowbar.'

'What did you find — emeralds and pearls belonging to the Spanish King?'

'If you're going to make a joke out of this, there's no point continuing,' Ross declared, leading her across the road when a car had passed.

'OK, I apologise.' She couldn't summon up much enthusiasm — ghosts, piracy, buried treasure! She was surprised Ross believed it all.

'In it were the original deeds to the property. Also, in a leather pouch which had deteriorated with age, were pieces of gold. Back then, they would have been worth a small fortune. My father contacted the authorities and after a long struggle, we were allowed to keep most of them.'

'I've never seen them.'

'Pop keeps his remaining ones locked away. When we reached our twenty-first birthday, he gave us two of them apiece. I don't know what Bill and Annetta have done with theirs. He said we could do with them as we wished.'

She had been so engrossed in their conversation, she was surprised to find they'd arrived at the house.

'Then what's happened to yours?' she asked with uncharacteristic nosiness.

His eyes regarded her necklace for a few moments then he confronted her surprised expression directly. Immediately her fingers went to the delicate chain.

'You didn't!' she exclaimed.

'I had you going there for a while, huh?' His laugh resounded around the covered entrance porch and she punched him playfully on the arm.

'I should know better than to believe anything you say, Roscoe Hamilton! You're the rogue of the family, not your innocent seafaring ancestor.'

They were still both laughing when Charles led them through to the formal dining room.

Annetta, who was sitting on the far sofa next to her father, leaped up and rushed across the room. She hugged Ross tightly.

'I didn't believe it when Daddy rang and told me.'

Ross pulled away slightly from her embrace. 'I hear there's a new addition to the family and Joshua must have grown some.' He looked around the room but only Annetta's husband, Philip, was there.

'You'll see them tomorrow. Joshua is dying to see you,' she added enthusiastically. 'We thought it would be better to leave them with their nanny.' Her concerned glance went from Ross to Emma.

'You needn't have worried. There'll be no more dreadful scenes,' he assured her with a winning smile.

After shaking Philip's hand, he returned to Emma's side and slid his arm around her waist. Instinctively, she moved into his warmth.

'All the same, I can understand why you were hesitant,' he went on. 'This afternoon, Pop and I made our peace, and now you can see for yourself that Emma and I are trying to get things sorted out between us.'

The material of Annetta's jade silk suit made a rustling sound as she hurried to them and embraced them both.

'I'm so happy. I've never seen two people more suited — haven't I always said that, Philip?' she declared, turning to her husband for confirmation.

'You have, yes,' he replied indulgently, smiling at her.

'I knew you two couldn't be kept apart. It was plain for anyone to see how much you loved one another,' she said tutting.

'Hey, slow down, sis,' Ross ordered her in a kindly way. 'Emma and I have a long way to go yet.'

'But I thought — '

'So will a lot of others and we can do without pressure from anyone. It's something we're going to have to sort out alone.'

Annetta reached out and grasped an arm of each of them.

'If there's anything we can do, we're here for you.'

'So when can I see my godson?' Ross beamed.

'Why don't you both come for supper tomorrow?' Annetta suggested eagerly. 'You'll have time to play with him before he goes to bed.'

'I can't answer for Emma. She may already have something planned for tomorrow,' he remarked.

'I usually go to my aerobics class on Monday evenings,' she told them. 'But I suppose I could miss it this week.'

'You don't have to cancel it on my

account,' Ross insisted in such a tender way that there was no contest.

'Can I ring you tomorrow, Annetta? I'll have to let my friend know I'm not going first.'

'We don't eat until late,' her sister-in-law countered. 'And we don't mind waiting, do we? I'll prepare something which won't spoil.'

Emma's necklace caught her eye.

'This is beautiful. Finally I get to see it for real.' Reaching out her long fingernails she tentatively touched it.

'Ross gave it to me,' Emma explained, puzzled.

'I know. He asked me if you'd like the design as we have similar tastes, you and I. He wanted a second opinion before he went to the jeweller to have it made up from a sketch.'

'A sketch?' Emma was astounded — Annetta had to be wrong. He wouldn't have gone to so much trouble for her.

'I wish Philip would take as much

78

trouble over my Christmas presents,' she whispered conspiratorially. 'Though he's a sweetheart, and I wouldn't swap him. It's more personal when someone has a gift made specially.'

Again Annetta glanced over her shoulder to see if the men were still safely at a distance and her actions were making Emma feel increasingly nervous.

'I thought he'd have wanted you to return it when you split up. Did he give it back to you today?'

'Why?' Emma asked her. 'Does it matter?'

'It's not for me to speak out of place, plus it's rather nasty to discuss money, but I'll warn you now as my brother seems to have forgotten. If I were you, I'd guard that piece of jewellery with my life.'

Emma bowed her head and regarded the necklace with fresh eyes. Weren't they just diamond chips, she pondered silently.

'Ross presented it to me today. He

found it tucked away in his closet this afternoon.'

'In his closet? I think not, Emma. Family safe, yes, definitely!'

'I don't understand,' she murmured. 'Why did he lie to me?'

'Perhaps he didn't want to show you just how serious he is about getting back together in case he scared you off.' Annetta's fingers traced the outline of her married initials. 'But knowing my brother as well as I do and what this is worth, I'd say he's mighty serious about your reconciliation!'

6

'What were you and Annetta talking about this evening?' Ross enquired as he walked her home. 'You were very subdued afterwards.'

'Was I?' she rejoined innocently, deliberately opening her eyes wide as she confronted him. 'Tiredness has caught up with me.'

'Do you think you'll make it to the bank on time in the morning?'

'I've promised to be there. I'll set my alarm to make sure I am.' It had been such a pleasant evening, even though Annetta's statement still had her reeling and she didn't want to consider what the next few days would hold, especially when Ross found out it was her name on the pay sheets.

Closing her eyes for a second as the earth suddenly spun wildly, his arm quickly caught her when she staggered.

'What's wrong?' he asked, holding her tighter.

'I'll be fine.'

'You don't look it! Your face is ashen, Emma. Here, sit down for a minute.'

'I'm sorry,' she pleaded.

'Shush! just relax.' He comforted her as her wave of nausea dissipated to nothing.

'But I feel so silly sitting here!'

'We're not moving until you're well enough to continue and I don't care what anyone thinks! If anyone is to blame for this, it's me. I should've known you were exhausted and I shouldn't have pressed you into such a harrowing evening.'

Ross reached over and stroked her cheek with his fingertips. Not only did his gesture surprise her, but it filled her with an overwhelming desire to be brought into his firm embrace.

'Why did it go so wrong, Em?' he asked, sadly. She couldn't tear her gaze from the pools of green speckled with amber — like autumn colours of a South Carolina forest on a brilliant October morning.

Instead of waiting for her reply, his lips came down on hers and his kiss was pure heaven. It wasn't for Thomas's benefit this time — it was just for her. Her arms slowly went around his neck as their kiss deepened. Her old love's flames had definitely been rekindled, she considered, savouring his taste on her lips.

All too soon, his ardour would be doused for ever. She pulled away knowing it was going to be more painful than their last separation.

He drew her face around with his hand and studied her.

'We got so caught up in our feud, we've both forgotten how good it could be between us. Will you do something for me, Em?'

'That depends on what it is,' she replied cautiously.

'Don't wear your ring yet. It seems it's brought nothing but trouble and I don't want to tempt fate. Call me superstitious if you will, but everything started to go wrong when I slipped that band of gold on to your finger.'

Clasping her hand in his, he brought it to his lips and kissed each finger in turn.

She smiled at him.

'We both suddenly had a lot of responsibilities which we didn't have before. Saying we were getting married was one thing, but actually going through with it . . . '

He nodded his agreement.

'In a short space of time, everything changed and well, here we are again, strangers who are attracted to one another, pretending to be in love. We've come full circle.'

She didn't like to remind him that there were a few matters he was forgetting: the biggest being his on-going relationship with Lindy. And how long would it be before Ross was accusing her of being more interested in Thomas and the business than him?

She'd practically admitted it to him to save face!

'I guess I shouldn't presume too much just because I've returned here to what's now your home town.'

'Would it be the same if I'd moved to Orlando?' she enquired cagily, scared his good mood would end.

'It's difficult to say,' he said, shrugging his shoulders. 'The pressures wouldn't be the same. Perhaps we should discuss this when we've sorted out the company troubles. Meanwhile, we'll keep up a united front when we have to meet the family. And if you still want to go to your aerobics class ... '

'Well, I'd thought about it but I'd be quite happy to go with you to Annetta's, if you want me there.'

His beaming smile had her pulse reacting in a strange way.

'I'd like it very much.' He pecked a kiss on her forehead. 'Are you feeling strong enough for the rest of the walk home?'

On arriving at her house, Ross

declined her offer of coffee.

'You really need some sleep,' he insisted as she unlocked the front door.

She turned to face him and smiled.

'I've had a great evening and thank you again for your present.'

Her senses swam when he kissed her, holding her to his body and she was surprised as he pulled away first. Kissing the tip of his middle finger, he then placed it on her lips.

'Until the morning.'

Hugging her arms around her, she stood at her lounge window and looked at the street below where he'd been, wishing he'd change his mind and return to her flat.

She strode away for three paces then back, raking her fingers through her tussled hair. Did he mean what he said — that he was attracted to her? But it was obvious the marriage didn't work out — and what of Lindy?

'Oh damn you, Ross Hamilton!' she cried, pummelling the nearest scatter cushion. 'Twenty-four hours and I'm like putty in your hands! I was supposed to deliver a message, get you back with your father and nothing more!'

She flopped down into an armchair and carefully undid the clasp of her new necklace. The small diamonds glittered in the light as she admired it. Would it be safe for her to leave it in the flat or should she make an excuse to put it in her safety box at the bank in the morning?

Yawning, she got up and hid her gift under her pillow before getting ready for bed. It had been a very long, eventful day and if she was lucky, the following one would be a lot less dramatic than she anticipated.

★   ★   ★

The bell was persistent as it sliced through her dreams. Emma reached out to turn off the alarm, the clock falling on to her carpet with her clumsiness, but the noise continued.

She was drowsy with sleep and she battled to regain full consciousness. Now there was banging, nearer to her. Struggling out of bed, she grabbed her wrap and threw it on as she staggered blindly across her lounge.

'Who is it? What do you want?' she called out huskily, tying the thin belt at her waist.

'It's Ross.'

She unlocked the door and opened it.

'What time is it?' she muttered, stretching and wishing she could have a few more hours of rest.

'Twenty minutes after the time you were due at the bank!'

'Oh, I'm sorry.' She collapsed into the nearest armchair. 'I haven't over-slept since I joined Hamiltons.'

Standing with his hands on the hips of his dark grey trousers, Ross took control.

'Go and get under the shower. There'll be coffee waiting for you when you come out.'

Standing under the icy cold needles

of water wasn't the best way to wake up, Emma thought as they stung her skin, but it was the quickest. After drying herself and slipping into a cool cream linen dress that was suitable for the office, she returned to find Ross had kept to his word about the coffee.

'Thanks for not getting annoyed, Ross. I don't normally break my promises.'

'I know — I found it an effort to get out of bed, too,' he said, smiling over at her. She doubted he had lay awake half the night going over the events of the last days as she had.

He went on, 'I've also contacted the office. I spoke to Marshall's secretary and asked her to tell him we'd be in later as we had company business to attend to.'

Her stomach churned. Marshall — she'd arranged to have lunch with him today. Could she remain sufficiently indifferent in her attitude over Ross when they'd shared those intimate moments yesterday evening?

Ross looked so handsome in his elegantly-cut suit and maroon tie opposite her, yet she knew beneath his business-like exterior beat his passionate heart and it thrilled her.

'That means the rumours will be already spreading through the office,' she said, getting up to find her handbag and making sure her keys were in it. As an afterthought, she slipped her new necklace into its back pocket.

Ross was lazing back in his chair when she returned, deep in thought.

'Can't his secretary be trusted then?'

'She seems OK,' she mused, guessing that Ross was trying to find out their weak link. 'Though she'll probably pass that snippet on to her best friend. They know you're Thomas's son and they'll all be wondering what you're doing here.'

'As you know them all well, maybe you should be on the look-out today to see who's acting suspiciously or slightly out of character. If they're shocked, it may give us the lead we need.'

She doubted it but didn't tell him. Whoever it was, they were playing it very cool indeed.

'I'm ready,' she informed Ross, putting on her linen jacket which matched her dress. 'Do you want to follow me in your car? I need to go into town with mine later on, anyway.'

Luckily he didn't get time to see her blush deepening as she busied herself locking up the flat before following him downstairs. She always insisted that she and Marshall took separate cars and today would be no exception.

Driving several times around the block where the bank was situated, Emma eventually found a spot to park in. When she arrived at the bank's entrance, Ross was waiting for her.

'Sorry — it took me a while to get parked. Town's particularly busy today,' she told him as they strolled inside into the cool, air-conditioned building and headed for the teller who dealt with the safety deposits.

Ross waited in the main lobby for her

as she was escorted into the room. A few minutes later, she returned with the ledger in her arms while her necklace was now secured with her important personal documents in the vault.

'I've got everything you need,' she told him in a hushed voice.

'Is there a coffee shop around here where we can go?'

'The old one's still there if that's what you mean,' she said as they strolled in the direction of one nearby that had been in business for many years.

As they slid into one of the booths at the back of the premises, an older woman came to greet them.

'Well, I'll be darned — Roscoe Hamilton!'

'Yes, ma'am, I'm back,' he beamed his reply.

'Oh my, you look more handsome. I'd better warn my friends to lock up their daughters.' Suddenly she realised Emma was sitting quietly opposite him and she blushed. 'I'm sorry, honey, I didn't mean anything by it.'

'It's OK,' Emma replied, smiling. 'I think it's the smart shirt that does it.'

Having taken their order, the woman hurried away.

'I can't remember who knew we were married and who didn't,' she whispered to him and passed the book to him.

'It's too late to worry now.' He shrugged, opening the ledger and studying his father's careful columns of figures. 'When did you say the discrepancies started?' He swivelled the book slightly so she could read it.

'Here,' she said and pointed to a date eight weeks ago. 'I double-checked them and before then they seemed to balance.'

He glanced at the computer print-out which she'd slipped into the back of it.

'And you said Pop had some other papers? They don't seem to be here.'

'I put them in my bag at the bank,' she declared, withdrawing them from the large pocket and passing them over the table. 'See, this is his handwriting.'

Picking them up, Ross put them inside the book then closed it firmly.

'I'll take them over to the accountant's office as soon as we leave here. It's just down the block. If we're lucky, we should have some idea today of what's involved.'

She could tell him the exact amount — and it was a frightening one! The thing she didn't know was how they'd got the extra money because the company to whom she'd authorised payment wasn't chasing her for money which she knew they would if they hadn't got it. It just didn't make sense. Hopefully the accountant would dig deeper into the matter.

'Pop told me a few things yesterday, but I'd like you to go over with me what's going on at the office right now.'

The woman brought their coffee and a much-needed plate of buttered toast for Emma. Between mouthfuls, she told him of their current projects and of who was dealing with the straightforward house sales and property leasing.

'And that's about it.' She sighed, pushing aside her empty plate and cup. 'I don't think there's anything I've left out.'

Her comment was met with a beaming smile.

'I can understand why Pop trusts you. You have everything under control.'

Everything except her reeling emotions, she mused wryly when her pulse began to race again as he reached over and covered her hand with his, giving her a tender squeeze.

'Will you mind acting as my Personal Assistant? I don't want to have to transfer you to another section, but if you think you can't work with me, we should discuss our options right now.'

It would be painful being so close to him and having to be business-like about their relationship yet she didn't want to be demoted when she'd toiled to achieve her current status.

'I'll be devoting some time on the retirement project. I only passed my workload over to another girl when Thomas became ill. If possible, I'd like to take it back to see it through to the end.'

'Then we'll do that. Let's see how it goes and maybe next weekend we can thrash out the details so we're both satisfied. After a week in the office, I should be back in the swing of things.'

'And you'll be wishing you were shooting at the good guys in Orlando again!' she joked as he escorted her outside.

'We'll see,' he replied, enigmatically. He patted the book tucked under his arm. 'Tell Marshall I'll want to see him. I should be back there in an hour.'

Smiling, he leaned forward and kissed her on the forehead.

She took a deep breath while she watched him stroll down the pavement, dodging the tourists. When had she realised she was in love with him? Walking slowly to where her car was parked, she tried to recall that precise moment when she'd admitted it to herself.

In a dream, she drove to the outskirts of town where the Hamilton premises were situated. Parking in her usual spot, she got out and locked her door. She knew now. It was that day the family had spent on the beach. A smile curled the corners of her lips.

Stretched out on her towel, she'd watched Ross playing with his nephew in the shallows, hearing their shared peals of laughter. They had run back to her with Joshua's bucket and had tipped its contents over her. Squealing, she leaped up and grabbed Ross, hoping to punch him playfully.

Instead he'd pulled her into his embrace, disarming her with a long kiss. Pulling her head away, she suddenly regarded him in a different light. He, too, was staring at her in a peculiar way. For the rest of the day, the atmosphere had been strained between them.

★ ★ ★

Emma strode to the entrance and flung open the door. She had to forget the past and get on with business. Cheerfully greeting the women and men who worked on house sales at the front desks, she made her way to the offices at the rear. Reaching Marshall's closed door, she paused for a few seconds but decided to see him when her pulse had resumed its usual rate.

A pot of coffee had been made by their secretary and was steaming on its hot plate. Shrugging off her jacket and hanging it over her chair, she went to pour herself some. Leaning against the bookcase as she cupped it in her hands, she studied the office which, until now, she'd shared with Thomas.

She was tidying the top of his desk when she heard the door open behind her. Emma glanced over her shoulder with forced nonchalance.

'Hi, Emma. I've just heard you were in,' Marshall said as he neared her.

With difficulty, she smiled at him.

'I was coming to see you in a minute. I wanted to get things straightened up.' Avoiding his outstretched hand, she hurried to her desk and sat down.

Perching on the edge of Ross's desk, he looked at her.

'What's going on? My secretary had a call earlier from Roscoe Hamilton. What's he doing here?'

'I'm sure he'll fill you in on everything. He'll be back soon and he wants to talk with you.'

'That sounds pretty ominous. What's the prodigal son like?'

She could say a lot, she mused, but replied, 'I'll let you make up your own mind. How did the concert go?'

'You'll kick yourself that you missed it.' He gave her details and she smiled as she listened.

'I'm sorry I let you down.' She didn't hide the guilt she was feeling. Marshall had become a good friend, though she could never think of him anything more than a platonic friend. He'd kissed her once, on their last date, and she hadn't felt that wonderful heady sensation she experienced when Ross's lips met hers.

'I took another friend along. She really enjoyed it.'

'Then I'm glad my ticket wasn't wasted,' she replied, uncertain if Marshall was trying to make her feel jealous. 'I had to fly down to Florida and tell Ross about his father.'

'Wouldn't it have been easier to phone him?' he snapped.

'He and Thomas used to be very close. As I'm a friend of their family, it seemed only fair I should inform him in person.'

Marshall was aware of her friendship with Thomas but he'd never been told the full story. Some things were best kept quiet from outsiders.

'But making you fly down there in your spare time,' he persisted.

'I chose to do it,' she retaliated sharply, pulling out a file from her drawer. 'Now I should get on with my work — I've wasted enough time already this morning.'

'Are we still on for lunch?' he enquired, stopping at her door.

'Why not?' She sighed. 'One o'clock?'

'I'll get the sandwiches and I'll meet you down at the marina.'

Her mood didn't get any better before Ross arrived. Jacqui, the woman she'd temporarily delegated her project work to, was loathe to return it to her.

Standing over the woman's desk, she held her hand out.

'If you want me to take the matter to Mr Hamilton when he gets here, then I will,' Emma threatened in an unfamiliar manner.

She knew she'd raised a few brows by her outburst and for once, she didn't care. She stood firm, glaring down at the brunette who was several years older than herself.

'He won't be happy to be burdened with such a trivial matter on his first day, Jacqui.'

Eventually the woman relented and Emma went back into her office with the files containing her work, slamming the door after her.

Only minutes later, the door opened once again.

'What is it now?' she thundered. Immediately she wished the floor would swallow her up.

'I don't have a white flag with me to wave,' Ross remarked in jest although his tone didn't belie his concern. He closed the door. 'I wasn't prepared to enter a battle zone. What's going on? It's deathly quiet out there.'

'A small difference of opinion which has been sorted out,' she explained, rubbing her temples with her fingertips as she sat back from her paper-strewn desk. 'Do you want me to ring through to Marshall?'

Taking off his jacket, Ross sat in his father's chair and relaxed back into its soft, leather cushion.

'I'll go to his office so we can talk in private. You're obviously very busy and don't want to be disturbed.'

'That's OK. I'm having a few

problems with this lot,' she said indicating to her desk. 'I'll have to drive down to the complex as it may make more sense then.' Getting up, she put on her jacket then tidied her papers into a pile. 'I'll be back after lunch. There are a few messages I've left on your desk.'

Luckily she had a plausible reason for going out, she mused, picking up her handbag and car keys. Mentally she wasn't ready to begin a working relationship with him when her feelings of their personal one were so muddled.

'Em?' he called to her when she got to the door and she stopped to face him. 'Are you sure you want to come to Annetta's tonight?'

'Of course I do,' she replied, beaming, as she'd forgotten it with all that morning's wrangles.

'I'm glad,' he countered, giving her a knowing wink.

7

'Where on earth have you been?' Ross stormed when she returned to the office.

She'd had a pleasant lunch with Marshall in the park beside the marina and she'd tried to hide her feelings of elation from him. From what Marshall told her, Ross had explained everything so nicely that he wasn't made to feel as though he was being moved back to his lower job.

Ross got up and came from behind his desk as she closed their door.

'I told you I'd be back after lunch,' she insisted, looking him in the eye when he neared her. 'What's the matter?' she continued with as much innocence as she could muster.

'Don't play games with me. You know precisely what's wrong, Emma,' he thundered.

'People will hear you,' she retorted. 'These walls are paper thin.'

'I don't give a damn! After today, you won't be around to worry about your precious reputation.' She stared up at him in horror. 'And they'll know they're not going to have an easy ride while I'm in charge of the company.'

'Please, Ross, you have to listen to me — '

'To more of your lies? What have you done with the cash — stashed it away in your safety deposit box for a rainy day? How could you steal from my father when he's already given you so much, Emma? We both have — and this is how you repay us!'

Tears streamed down her cheeks at his amazing outburst and accusations and she fought to control her sobs.

'How long did you think it'd take an experienced accountant to find out what tricks you'd been playing, huh?' He ran his fingers through his hair as he seemed to be thinking.

'Please,' she begged, her body shaking from tremulous sobs. She caught his arm with her hand but he threw it from him, his mouth curling in disgust.

'Get out, Emma! Take your things and get out of here!'

Rooted to the spot, as her world crumbled around her, she cried, 'I'm innocent, Ross. Don't you see? I'd never hurt Thomas — never!'

'Save your excuses for the authorities. What a pity we signed a pre-nuptial agreement otherwise I may have received some of your ill-gotten gains in our divorce settlement.'

'You're divorcing me?' She staggered to her chair and collapsed into it.

'As soon as I can. I don't want anything more to do with you. I'm surprised my father put you in charge with Marshall, let alone welcome you into his house.'

'But doesn't that mean something to you, Ross? He knows I'm not to blame. Somebody has framed me.'

'Just go. You can return for your

things in the morning as I won't be here. I'll get Marshall to put them in a box for you.'

He didn't know it but that was the final insult. Grabbing her bag, she got up and confronted him with more strength now.

'I won't give you the satisfaction of divorcing me,' she spat out. 'I'm going straight down to my lawyer when I leave here and I'll be citing your little friend Lindy as co-respondent in a charge of adultery. She'll do among the many.'

'Emma, I wouldn't if I were you,' he warned her.

Her eyes blazed with fury.

'I've taken your affairs for long enough but I did it because you helped me when I needed it. I'll be glad when we're no longer man and wife — though the moment I'm really looking forward to is when you're going to have to eat humble pie. You'll see I'm innocent — and I can't wait!'

With a flourish, she left the office,

practically wrenching the door off its hinges. Marshall was standing by one of the front desks, pretending to be discussing business. Even those with phones to their ears were staring at her.

'You wanted to know what your new boss was like?' she called caustically across to Marshall. 'Well, now you know. Good luck because you're going to need it!'

It took a lot of inner strength not to break down and cry when she got in her car. Aware Ross and the others could be watching from the windows, she kept her chin held high as she drove towards town.

Too distraught now for a meeting with her lawyer, she returned to her flat and broke down in tears. More than once that afternoon she cursed the day she'd come to South Carolina.

★ ★ ★

Her telephone rang several times over the hours and eventually she took it off the hook. She didn't want to hear Marshall's comforting words down the line nor another verbal attack from her soon-to-be ex-husband.

How could she go to the office tomorrow morning? Just how much had they overheard? Would Marshall even want to know her still as a friend when she'd lied to him over her matrimonial state? The whole thing was a dreadful mess!

Crying herself to sleep, her head was thumping loudly when she came to. She dragged herself through to the bathroom to get some aspirins but the noise was coming from her door.

'Go away!' she shouted, wincing in pain.

'Emma, open this door!' Ross roared.

'Leave me alone,' she cried. 'Just go away.'

'I'll kick it in if I have to,' he warned through the wood and she knew he meant it.

Leaving the safety chain on, she unlocked the door and opened it a fraction. Her neighbour, Isabelle, was standing beside Ross and she was looking very worried.

'I let this gentleman in, Emma, because he told me you weren't well and you weren't answering the telephone.'

'I'm extremely sorry to have put you to so much trouble,' Emma remarked pointedly as she felt unable to confront Ross's glare directly.

'I knew you were in because I . . . em . . . heard you earlier!' The woman then stared at Ross. 'This gentleman says he's your husband.'

'Unfortunately, he is — at least for the moment. I promise we won't bother you again.' Closing the door to take off the chain, she opened it wide and her neighbour gasped when she saw Emma's dishevelled state.

'I've had some bad news today so I'm not quite myself,' she explained in a strained voice.

'Well, if there's anything you need, you know where we are.'

'My wife is lucky to have such concerned neighbours,' Ross interjected smoothly. 'I'll stay with her for a while until she's calmed down.'

Emma stood aside to let Ross enter, then assured the kind woman she'd be safe with him and agreeing she'd drop into their flat the next morning for a chat and coffee.

'Thanks a lot, Ross,' she hissed, striding past him to the kitchen to get herself a glass of water and take her painkillers. She felt his presence behind her when she swallowed the second one. 'You kick me out of the company then you practically get me booted out of my own home.' Eyes blazing, she confronted him and in a tired, flat tone demanded, 'Why don't you just leave me alone?'

He leaned against the door frame, his arms folded across his chest as he watched her. 'We didn't finish our conversation earlier on.'

'Funny.' She chuckled without any mirth. 'I recall you telling me to get out of your office, which I did. Subject closed.'

'You're not looking too great, Emma.'

'What did you expect? You refused to listen to me — you called me a thief,' she cried, her voice rising with hysteria.

'Calm down, Em. Have a seat and I'll make you some tea.'

She glowered at him, wondering why he was being so charming.

In the bathroom, she changed into her towelling lounging suit. At least she could discard her wrinkled dress but there wasn't much she could do for her bloodshot eyes and drawn features other than rinse them in cold water.

'I thought you were going to Annetta's,' she remarked, rejoining him. She had no idea of the time as she'd drawn her curtains, shutting out the world.

'I dropped by and told them I'd sent you home as you weren't feeling well. They understand I wanted to look after you,' he declared, coming to her where she sat curled up in an armchair and passing her a mug of tea.

'Aren't the lies ever going to stop?' she cried.

'What did you want me to tell them — that my wife could be charged for embezzling the family's money?'

'Have you come to gloat?' she asked, watching him as he sat opposite her.

'No. As soon as you left today, I knew things had gone too far. I tried to call you, Em.'

'I wasn't in the mood to chat,' she snapped, glaring at him.

'Why didn't you let me know the full story on Saturday or yesterday?'

'Because I knew what your reaction would be,' she replied, sipping her drink. It was just how she liked it. 'But I had to take the initiative to find you, even though I'd been implicated. I couldn't let this person rip off Hamiltons any longer. Your father's too weak to fight them but you can do it. If I was guilty, Ross, I would have packed up and got on the first plane back to England.'

'So Pop didn't ask you to come down for me?'

Blushing at being caught, she shook her head.

'It was my idea and he agreed to it,' she murmured then quickly insisted, 'although he'd been looking for an excuse to get you home.'

'I realise that. He and I had a long talk on Sunday afternoon and cleared the air. He said a few things which at the time didn't make sense but I didn't press him as he was becoming tired. After today's revelations, I'm beginning to understand what he was getting at. It seems he came to the same conclusion as myself, though it's taken me longer to get there.'

'Which is?' she prompted when he stopped to take a mouthful from his mug.

His eyebrows rose. 'That you were set up.'

'At last!' She cheered sarcastically, almost spilling her coffee. 'You put me through that humiliating scene at the office for nothing!'

'I know this sounds funny but it may work in your favour. The real thief will believe they're in the clear now that you've been fired. But I doubt they'll resign immediately in case it draws attention to them.' He withdrew a piece of paper from his inside pocket and opened it out, flattening its creases with his hand. Emma saw it was another computer print-out. 'This afternoon I went over the latest figures and I found something very surprising. You put through some payments at the end of last week — Marshall co-signed them for you.'

She thought back and then nodded.

'Yes, we continued to co-sign them for each other to keep Thomas happy.'

With his finger, he indicated to a particular amount of five thousand dollars.

'It's always the same company the money goes to.'

'The amount is wrong,' she insisted, reaching across to take the paper from him. 'It should be five hundred dollars.'

'Forget the amount, Emma. Look at the date it was typed into the computer.'

Her brow furrowed and, although her headache was barely a dull ache, her mind couldn't work out what date it was today.

Tutting impatiently, Ross sat back into the cushions.

'It's Saturday, Emma. It gives the time, too — five-fourteen in the afternoon. Honey, even you can't be in two places at once!' Her widened eyes met his. 'My show was scheduled to end a minute later.'

'Then it was someone who was working on Saturday?'

'It could be anyone who had a key to the office. Didn't you say that you've recently altered the opening hours?'

'Yes.' She sighed, wishing her mind was less foggy. 'We open on Sunday mornings now for a few hours and we close at four on Saturday.'

'If they were working, they'd have to

have had a good excuse to stay on and have a key to lock up afterwards. Failing that, they returned when everyone else had gone. Firstly, we have to find out if anyone wanted to do some overtime. Marshall was quick to defend you today, perhaps he's trying to cover himself.'

'No, I'm sure it's not him,' she declared. 'What did he say to you?'

'Let's just say that some things he said today would have got him fired under normal circumstances!' He chuckled. 'I told him I'd discuss it further when he'd had a chance to cool down.'

Green eyes bored into her and she felt heat rising to her pale cheeks.

'It's not Marshall,' she said quietly. 'He was at a concert on Saturday. We were supposed to be going there together.' Her skin was now aflame. 'It was an early evening performance in Charleston. And to get there for the start we'd had to have left here by four o'clock at the latest.'

'They were the tickets you were talking about on the phone?'

'Didn't anyone teach you that it's rude to eavesdrop?' she challenged then went on. 'I know he saw the performance because he gave me a blow-by-blow account this lunchtime. He hadn't seen the group before — I have, last summer in Savannah, and they haven't changed their act since then. You can trust Marshall.'

'But can I trust him with my wife?' he joked, with an underlying seriousness to his tone.

'Nearly ex-wife,' she reminded him. 'We haven't managed to discuss that yet.'

'Let's deal with one crisis at a time, Em! Do you have any bourbon left?'

'Help yourself. There's some in the cupboard,' she replied, gesturing towards the kitchen.

He returned a few minutes later, deep in thought.

'How often are the cheque runs?'

'Twice a week — on Wednesday and

Saturday mornings,' she answered, watching him as he swirled the amber liquid around the ice cubes. She stared up at him with excitement and met his smile. The special stationery used was locked away except for when it was needed for the printer.

They only had a small operation and it was always a hassle if anyone needed something urgently printed off when the cheque run was in progress on their main one which produced more professional looking documents.

'I was trying to get Thomas to have another laser printer installed!' she cried. 'Ross, it's still waiting on the system — they haven't got it!'

Relief surged through her veins and tears welled up in her eyes.

'It's not over yet,' he interceded seriously.

'But at least you're convinced I'm innocent,' she said, rubbing her stomach again as it growled. 'I'm sorry,' she explained with a smile.

'I'll call for a pizza delivery. Where's

your phone book?'

'They'll be here in twenty minutes,' he said, replacing the handset after giving their order. 'Meanwhile, we should consider what we're going to do. I don't want to get the police involved just yet, although I know we should. Pop is still pretty weak, even though he's doing his best to pretend he's fine.'

'It might help his recovery if he knows something is being done,' she insisted.

He glanced at his watch.

'It's too late tonight. Let's see what tomorrow brings.'

'But tomorrow's Tuesday. The print run isn't until Wednesday,' she reminded him. 'And we don't know whether those cheques have been sent out in the post with the others.'

While they waited for the pizza van to arrive, Emma made a list of all the company's employees, including those who'd recently left in case they'd got a copy of the front door key. Over their much-needed meal, they went over the list, marking those people's names who they believed might have access or motive to do it.

'We haven't got very far.' She sighed, stifling a yawn as she cleared away the few, now cold, slices of pizza they hadn't been able to manage.

'Get some sleep,' Ross ordered, helping her clear away. 'You know what to do in the morning?'

'Yes. I wait down the road from the office in my car until I see you leave. You've taken part in too many detective films, Ross. Nobody does that in real life!' Emma shook her head in disbelief.

'Look, if I get an urgent call when I'm about to leave, I can hardly say to them, 'I have to go as it's dead on ten o'clock and my wife is about to make her theatrical entrance.' This way, you'll see me go and know it's safe. And remember, put on just enough make-up so it looks like you're trying to hide your humiliation.'

'That won't be difficult,' she remarked, standing to face him. 'You made me feel this big,' she chided him, her thumb and forefinger closing to an inch of each other.

His hand cupped her shoulder and squeezed it. 'I'm so sorry about that, honey. When this is over, you have my assurance I'll make it up to you. Everyone will be informed that we staged it purposely to find the perpetrator. Now, you've got everything straight in your mind?'

'Yes, yes, of course I have.' Emma was now exasperated with Ross. She sometimes felt he treated her as if she was a little girl.

'Just do as I've told you,' he replied sternly. 'And I'll meet you at the marina at midday.'

★ ★ ★

Waiting in her car, she felt like a character from one those old films that she loved to watch. If only she could be back at her flat now, she mused, glancing again at her watch. It was a minute to ten. Her hands were trembling from her rising nervousness.

Having awoken at seven, after a fitful night's sleep, she didn't have to play-act at appearing distraught — she looked dreadful.

Staring up the road she could see Ross's red sports car approaching. He stopped alongside her car and his automatic window wound down.

'You look terrible — you've done a great job!' he beamed at her. 'I've had a call and I may be a few minutes late so wait at the marina for me.' Before she could reply, his car sped off down the road.

The next minutes of waiting were nerve-racking. Their plan was in action and now Emma had to act as she never had before! She had to pull it off. Everything was riding on this performance.

Though hadn't she been able to in the past? Ross had no idea she'd loved him, nor how she was feeling now. Should she tell him the truth at long last, regardless that she would look a fool?

Driving carefully to the building, she noticed someone had left their vehicle in her usual spot so she parked next to Marshall's on the far side.

From outside, she heard the regular hectic noise of their office but when she opened the door and went in, it ceased immediately.

'Can you get Marshall for me, please?' she asked the girl sitting nearest to her, biting her quivering lips for effect. She caught the girl's arm as she got up from her chair. 'Is Mr Hamilton here?' she added in a tremulous whisper.

'You've just missed him. He's had to go to the airport so he won't be back for a while yet,' the girl informed her in a kindly manner. 'I'll get Marshall for you.'

Nodding, Emma turned away and pretended to study the aerial photograph of the retirement project hanging on the wall. At her side, her hands formed into clenched fists. She wasn't going to let them take this from her: she'd worked hard and she was going to be at the celebratory dinner, completely exonerated of the charges of theft.

A hand touched her shoulder and she spun around. 'Marshall!' she sobbed, throwing herself towards him and he caught her in his arms.

'Someone get Emma a coffee!' She didn't pull her head up to see if they'd obeyed but judging from the noise she guessed they had. 'Come through to my office.'

'He might come back,' she pleaded. 'I couldn't — ' Howling to cut off anything more, she let him lead her through the desks as she dabbed at her eyes with a soggy tissue. Her tears were very real. She'd remembered the hatred in Ross's voice when he told her he was divorcing her.

After helping her to a chair, he took the cup which a woman brought in to him. The tears were burning her skin and, gazing up through the mist, she nodded her thanks to Jacqui.

'I tried to call you yesterday,' Marshall said when Jacqui had left the room. 'You weren't answering it and then it was engaged. I thought of coming to see you but reckoned you wouldn't want any visitors.'

'It was so humiliating,' she said as she took the coffee.

'That man is a pig! He knows exactly what I think of him after our little confrontation yesterday.'

'I'm surprised he didn't fire you on the spot, too!' she exclaimed. 'Though it was very sweet of you to defend me.'

Marshall sat on the desk in front of her. He seemed so concerned that she wanted to hug him and tell him the truth right this minute but she couldn't. In Ross's plan, that would come later.

'What was it about?' he asked, handing her a fresh handkerchief.

She blew her nose and wiped her cheeks.

'How much did you hear?'

'After his initial explosion, not a lot

— the occasional word, that's all.'

That's what they'd been counting on. She sighed deeply and shook her head.

'Please, Marshall, don't think badly of me. You've been wonderful and I don't want to lose your friendship.' She stopped for a few moments, to highlight she was in a dreadful quandary. 'There are some things I haven't told you and I should have. I tried to forget the past happened.'

'What is it?' he pleaded as she blew her nose.

She glanced at the door.

'We can't talk here. I'm scared he'll find us. Get my box of things and I'll meet you later. How about the marina again?'

'One o'clock?'

She shook her head emphatically.

'I have an appointment then. Will midday be OK?'

He nodded. 'I'll get your box now,' he said, getting up and leaving the office.

When he returned with it in his arms, the piece of paper she'd taken from his file was safely stored in her handbag.

'Twelve o'clock it is,' Marshall whispered then helped her to her car.

8

Marshall was five minutes early, she noted, seeing his car arrive in the carpark. He parked next to hers near the wall. Rising from the wooden bench, Emma went to greet him.

'You look better than you did earlier,' he remarked at her now dry-eyed face.

'Please don't hate me for what I'm about to tell you,' she insisted as they strolled to the grassy area where they'd had lunch on the previous day.

'I couldn't hate you, Emma.'

'You might.' Emma took a deep breath, 'Ross isn't just Thomas's son, he's my husband, too!' She said it quickly before she lost her courage.

'What?'

'We've been separated for a few years but neither of us has bothered to get a divorce.' Sitting together on a bench, she filled him in on the bare details then went on to tell him of the stolen money.

'Why didn't you tell me last week when you found out?' he demanded.

'Quite honestly, Marshall, I didn't know whom I could trust. I had to turn to Ross for help.'

'And he believes you're guilty?'

'Not any more and he knows you're innocent. I'm so sorry I had to use you this morning but we didn't know how you'd react if you knew the truth.'

'You both played me for a fool!'

'No!' she insisted. 'You were marvellous. We couldn't let the thief think we know what is going on concerning the missing money.'

'You know who it is?' Marshall waited for an answer.

'Not yet.' She stared at the ground and her cheeks burned. 'You might be told at some point, but yesterday's argument was for real.'

'I have to tell you, divorce was one of the words I overheard. No wonder you didn't want anything more to do with him.' Marshall shook his head slowly.

'I still love him, Marshall. I've only seen him lose his temper twice now and both times he's had cause to. When you get to know him, Ross is a very kind, loving man who has the utmost loyalty towards his family.'

'Yet you let him shout at you like that!'

'When I went to Florida on Saturday, I knew we'd come to blows. We have a long history and it all came to a head at the office yesterday. I was just as bad. I said things I shouldn't.'

'So you're not divorcing him?'

'I don't know,' she mused aloud. 'I really don't know.'

'But you don't want a relationship with me, is that it?' Marshall asked, sadly.

'You've been a great friend and I hope it won't be spoiled now you know the truth. Maybe I led you on — '

'You didn't,' he reassured her, squeezing her arm. 'It was wishful thinking on my part. You acted with propriety — for a married woman.'

'Just one more thing.' She spoke gently. 'I don't want anyone at the office to know who my husband is.' She glanced at her watch.

'What's up?' Marshall asked.

'Ross was supposed to be meeting us down here. He wants to speak to you now you know all the facts. We can go through this,' she said, taking out the previous week's work sheet she'd taken from Marshall's desk.

'Why didn't you ask me for it at the office?' he snapped. 'You didn't believe me, did you?'

'I did, but I couldn't ask for it and give the game away.' In the distance she saw a flash of red in the car park. 'Here he is. So much for telling me to be on time!'

'Emma, before he gets here, who is precisely divorcing whom?'

Her brow furrowed.

'To be honest, I don't know if he meant it any more than I did. Why?'

'Because I don't want to see you get hurt.'

Ross was strolling down the path towards them.

'What do you mean?' she hissed.

'If he's divorcing you, I think maybe he's already found a replacement wife.'

'What are you talking about?'

'I passed him in town on the way here. He was standing by that flash car of his and he was kissing some young woman. Sorry,' he added, wincing.

'You won't say anything to Ross, will you, Marshall — not after I've told you how I still feel about him?'

She was close to tears again as Ross caught up with them.

'Have you told him everything?' Ross enquired, sitting next to her.

'Oh, yes, we've had a very enlightening discussion,' she retorted, sardonically. 'I've nearly lost a friend this morning but I think he's forgiven me.'

'Good. I see you have the work list. Here's the one we drew up last night,'

Ross said getting it from his pocket. 'You were working on Saturday, Marshall. Who was with you?'

For the next hour, they discussed every employee, dismissing several who were definitely out of the area, including the girl whom Marshall had taken to the concert in Emma's place.

'She's very nice,' Emma remarked without rancour then passed on to the next name.

'Are we getting any closer?' Marshall groaned and got up to stretch his legs. 'I should get back. I'm already late.'

'We'll go back together and make out that you've been showing me around Emma's complex. I wanted to see it before it's fully open.'

Lies came so easily to Ross that it frightened Emma. Sitting on the kerb that evening, he'd said he wanted her — but obviously not that much. Her eyes narrowed angrily. Now he had another woman in tow he wouldn't be needing Emma anymore.

'What do you want me to do?' she enquired flatly.

'Go home and get some rest. If you're not busy tonight, Marshall, could you come to my father's house at eight?'

'Do you want me, too?' Emma cut in.

'No, we'll be needing you bright-eyed tomorrow. I want you to arrive at the office at ten o'clock again. You're not going to be very pleased about it either,' he informed her.

'Isn't that the truth!' she retaliated, annoyed he was now casting her aside.

'I've called you in to train your replacement. I'm sure we can trust you to do a convincing job, Emma.'

'Don't patronise me. I might just contest our prenuptial agreement after all!'

Ross chuckled deeply and she strode in a blaze of fury to her car, ignoring his calls for her to return.

★   ★   ★

'Is Mr Hamilton in?' Emma enquired, confronting the girl whom Marshall had dated on Saturday. 'He rang me and asked me to come in,' she snapped.

'Yes, he's in his office. I'll call through and make sure he's not busy.'

'I know the way, thank you.' Emma's eyes narrowed and her grip over her handbag tightened.

Emma went straight into the office without knocking but stopped dead on the threshold. A woman, with very long legs showing beneath her minuscule skirt, was draped across her husband's desk. The brunette's tousled, yet stylish hairstyle was more than a bit familiar to Emma.

Lindy turned on hearing Emma's forced cough and Ross got to his feet.

'I'm pleased you were so prompt. I don't have to introduce you two.'

Emma's lips drew into a thin grimace as she nodded.

'I asked you here to train your replacement.'

'You are joking, I hope! Her?' In her

shock, Emma forgot her manners.

'Lindy does have a name you know.' Ross's voice was cold.

'I know a few choice names I'd like to call both of you right now! Forget it! I'm not training your mistress!'

'You want me to call the police? I'll do it, Emma. The only reason I've not had you charged before now is because you're my wife.'

'Why don't you get a loud-hailer? Someone in Charleston might not have heard you!'

'You see what I had to contend with?' he declared, turning to Lindy who was smiling. 'And you wondered why our marriage fell apart?'

'I'm going,' Emma thundered but before she could take a step, Ross had caught hold of her by the arms.

'It will take two hours at the most,' he insisted. 'Please just do as I ask. Marshall has cleared a desk for you outside.'

'I won't — '

'Just do it, Emma.' Letting her go, he

strode outside and she watched as Lindy straightened herself.

'You love him, don't you?' the brunette said as she reached Emma and gazed down at her.

Emma straightened her back to give herself extra height.

'What makes you think that?' she snapped.

'Because it's written all over your face. I saw how you looked at him when you came to the apartment and again just now,' Lindy said without malice.

'I hope you can make him happier than I could.' Biting her bottom lip, Emma hurried away into the security of Marshall's office, only to be confronted there by Ross.

'Aren't you supposed to be showing Lindy the ropes?'

'I know what I'd like to do with those damned ropes!' she muttered angrily under her breath. 'I'm here to see if Marshall would like lunch with me today.'

'Why don't you get on with what

we're paying you for?' Ross sighed, turning back to talk to Marshall.

'I'd . . . I'd . . . Oh, I give up!' With a toss of her head, she flounced into the open-plan office.

She was in too deep to ever hope of returning here. As much as she wanted to apologise to everyone in turn for her ghastly behaviour of late, how could she work alongside Ross's new girlfriend?

'I'll go through these files with you first,' Emma said joining Lindy.

'This is the complex you mentioned?' Lindy jabbed a painted nail at a photograph. The brunette's words cut her to the quick.

'Yes, now this is what I've done so far.'

While Emma went through everything, she felt Lindy wasn't listening to her as carefully as she should. At least Emma had originally been employed for her good typing and shorthand speeds and not as a decoration to amuse the boss.

'Will you excuse me for a few

minutes?' Lindy asked and hurried off.

Why is everybody so impolite around here, she fumed silently, raising her eyebrows in agreement when one of the secretaries pulled a sympathetic face.

Within a few minutes, Lindy was back.

'Ross wants to see you in his office,' she purred smugly, sitting down and poring over a file.

This time Emma knocked on his open door and he glanced up. He was talking on the telephone.

'Sit down,' he whispered to her, covering the mouthpiece. He turned away from her. 'Yes, we'll see you there.' He swivelled back and put the receiver down. He opened his top drawer and withdrew an envelope.

'There's no need for you to stay on any longer, Emma. Lindy seems to know what's happening and if she has any queries then I'm sure Marshall will be pleased to assist.' He held out the envelope to her. 'This is for your help today. I know my father would want you to have it.'

'I don't want your money,' she spat out, refusing to take it from him. 'Over the past three years, I've learned to stand on my own feet. Whatever I decide to do now, I'm not going to be beholden to anybody. I'm going to ask Thomas one last favour and that's a reference from him.'

'You want him to give you a glowing report after all you've done?' he stormed, glaring over her shoulder at the open door. 'You've got a nerve, lady.'

Emma leaped to her feet.

'I'm going to see him right now and you're not going to stop me!'

In a flash, Ross was around the desk and he caught her arms in his hands.

'What are you playing at, Emma?' he hissed, looking very worried.

'I could ask you the same thing,' she whispered in retaliation. 'I thought I still had a job here then suddenly your fancy woman turns up and I'm out! I can't take any more. I'm going to tell your father I've decided to move elsewhere.'

'You're settled here — Beaufort is your home,' he insisted, his fingers gripping her.

'No, it's your home. I'll go either to Charleston or Savannah. I'm sure I'll settle down quickly in either of them. And it's time I met some new people.' She lifted her chin proudly. 'I'm not the insecure girl I was when your father came to England. I've done a lot of growing up — I've had to.'

'Emma, about the divorce — '

'Don't worry, I won't be citing Lindy and I won't contest it. I'll forward my address on to Thomas. He'll know where you have to send your papers.'

'Emma, we have to discuss this,' he persisted.

'It's too late.' Her mind was already made up. There were too many ghosts in Beaufort, and the only way she could begin to exorcise them was to leave. 'I'm going to see Thomas now.'

The phone on his desk rang. From

the chime she knew it was an internal call.

'Just wait a second,' he implored, hurrying and snatching up the receiver. 'Yes? Right now? Yes, I'm on my way.'

His fingers raked his hair as he turned to Emma.

'I have to go. I can't explain.' He grabbed his car keys from his desk and strode back to her. 'Don't do anything rash, Emma. Wait for me at Pop's.' His hands grasped her arms and he shook her for emphasis. 'Promise me!'

Stunned, she nodded and he flew out of the office. Wondering what was going on, she turned to the main office where the employees who weren't busy with telephone calls were standing at the window. Intrigued, Emma joined them finding a gap only to see Lindy and Ross by his car. Her body tensed as she noticed his arm was around the brunette's waist.

'Hey, what's happening?' one of the young men from sales called out when he finished his call.

Emma turned away and immediately bumped into Marshall. She didn't want to see her husband cuddling another woman in full view of everyone. To hang with her promise!

'I'll call you tonight, Marshall,' she informed him flatly. 'I may need to ask you a favour or two, if you don't mind.'

'No, of course not.' He sounded puzzled.

Standing on tiptoe, she kissed his cheek.

'Thanks, you've been a great friend.' His expression of concern deepened at her tone of finality. 'I'll be in touch.'

Fortunately, the embracing couple had gone and so had the sleek red sports car when she got outside. Close to tears she refused to let herself go as she drove directly to Thomas's house. Later, when this was all behind her, she would let herself wallow in self-pity as she decided on her future.

* * *

Thomas rose from his seat in the garden when Charles showed her through.

He pecked Emma on the cheek.

'You're looking much better,' she declared as he continued to hold her hands in his.

'I wish I could say the same for you and that son of mine,' he replied, raising a grey brow while he regarded her. 'Though I don't think my physician could do anything to help either of you. Would you like something to eat?'

'No, I'm fine,' she fibbed only to be confronted by a stern glance.

He called over his shoulder, 'Charles, can you get Emma some shrimp and salad? And we'll have some tea as well, thank you.'

Taking the seat next to his at the table, Emma started to talk.

'Ross was telling me about your family. The original Hamilton, William, sounded a real scallywag.'

'It depends which version you choose to believe,' he said laughing. 'There are many tales which over the years have been romanticised. Although one point seems to have remained constant — he had the utmost loyalty to his wife whatever mischief he may have got up to. It may sound boastful for me saying this, but I do believe that same loyalty has been passed down through the Hamilton family genes.'

'I don't think you're boasting. You loved your wife very much.'

'Don't get me wrong — it doesn't mean I haven't considered remarrying since she died as I do miss female companionship, but I haven't found a woman I've felt I could be loyal to. Do you understand?'

'Yes, I do,' Emma replied, nodding.

'Take my children,' he went on, conjuring up the memories. 'Bill — he met his sweetheart at High School and there was never any doubt in his mind. Annetta, well, she's very much like her mother in her ways yet she has the same Hamilton streak. As for Ross, well . . . '

He chuckled while Charles brought

them their tray of drinks and Emma's lunch plate.

When Charles left, she prompted, 'What about Ross?'

'He's just like the old man reincarnated! He knows his own mind and won't always take well-meaning advice. The story goes that William was warned of the storm but he still went out that night for the sake of his family, for one last run before he retired.'

'Run?' she enquired, picking up a large prawn in her fingers and nibbling it.

'He was running rum down to Savannah. In those days, rum was banned by the Trustees of the new British colony of Georgia. His ship was wrecked just off this coast.'

'I didn't believe Ross when he told me,' she said.

'It's the version I prefer as it highlights what a Hamilton man would do. In the present day it must sound pretty chauvinistic.'

'Not at all,' she declared between

mouthfuls. 'Although I think men and women should be equals, I'd love to have a man show me how much he loved me.'

'Maybe you haven't been looking closely enough,' he contended and she blushed profusely. 'I saw Annetta admiring your necklace the other evening.'

'It was a gift from Ross.'

'Yes, I know. I hope one day you'll have a daughter so you can pass it on to her. Usually boys don't treasure family heirlooms as girls do.'

She laid down her knife and fork.

'Thomas, I don't want to sound as if I'm a gold-digger but perhaps you will tell me the truth because Annetta has been hinting while Ross has kept silent about it. I'm scared to have it in my possession so I've put it in the bank.'

'I'd say that was a wise move on your part. Ross came to me and asked my permission to have the gold made up into a necklace for you.'

She sat back in her chair in astonishment.

'It was the gold that was found — '

'Yes, he told me about it but I didn't believe him,' she cut in.

'For him to do that, I knew he'd found somebody else he loved so I couldn't go against his wish as it was going to remain in the family, even though it wasn't in its original form.'

'Somebody else?' she echoed. She knew he'd only acted that way to stop his father realising their marriage was a sham.

'He's never told you?' Thomas sounded incredulous. 'Not to this day?'

Thomas leaned forward and poured tea into their cups.

'No wonder there's been so much bad blood between you — though you both seem to be working hard on a reconciliation. Perhaps Ross is wise to leave it in the past.'

'I'd like to know,' she insisted against her better judgement.

'OK.' He sighed. 'Though I'd have

preferred him to tell you himself as I can only tell you what I heard and saw. I can't say what turmoil my boy went through, only he can do that.

'Ross returned from California very suddenly. I've never seen him so withdrawn. He insisted he wanted to join the business because he'd had his fill of Hollywood. I'll give him his dues, he worked very hard at the office seven days a week. The family tried to help him but he refused our offers. We got some calls here from his friends in California, and again, he refused to take them.'

Emma sipped her tea to quench her parched mouth.

'When one came and he wasn't here, I got Charles to put the call through to my study. It was a woman — the mother of his girlfriend there — as I was led to believe at the time,' Thomas added, taking a sip of tea. 'In her own words, she said Ross was in no way to blame for the accident and that he'd still be welcome in their family's home.'

Emma listened in amazement.

'When he came back I confronted him with it and for the first time in his life he broke down. Even when he was young, he'd take everything on board, not like Bill. Anyhow, it seems the girl was his fiancée and she was in the same line as Ross.

'They met on a film set when he was put in charge of the second unit stunt team. Towards the end of shooting, she was killed while she was performing a stunt which Ross had devised. He was totally exonerated but he continued to blame himself for her death.'

'That's dreadful!' Emma cried.

'We couldn't make him see sense and it was only when you arrived that he seemed to be getting back to his former self. My family were shocked — though very pleased — when he told us he was getting married to you.

'Then when he asked permission for the gold to be remoulded, we realised he really was in love and he'd broken the vow he'd made in my study.'

'What had he said?' Her china cup was trembling noisily.

Thomas shrugged as if it was of no consequence.

'That he'd never marry for love.'

9

'Are you feeling OK?' Thomas enquired, leaning forward and touching her arm. 'You're rather pale.'

'Yes, yes,' she murmured in shock.

'But you've nothing to worry about, Emma,' he insisted gently. 'Ross does love you and I know you love him. If I'd tried to get in the way, though, it would have made everything worse. He'd have dug his heels in. The time had to be right — for both of you.'

She was glad of Charles's interruption as he came to take away her plate. She was still reeling from the shock that any hopes she may have had about Ross ever loving her were dashed.

It had been something for her to cling on to in this stormy passage called a marriage, that maybe — for just a fleeting moment even — Ross had felt love for her. But with recent events fresh in her mind then Thomas's explanation, she felt as if she was drowning in a swirling sea of emotion.

'Thomas, I have to tell you the truth,' she blurted out. 'The pretence can't go on any longer! I'm not supposed to be upsetting you,' she cried.

'Regardless of what my physician thinks, I'm feeling absolutely fine, so let me be the judge, Emma! I'm well aware you were accused of stealing that money. I saw the evidence for myself and I knew immediately you'd never do it.

'Yes, I admit we've been friends and friends' loyalty can sometimes waver, but you'd never steal from the family of the man you loved.'

'Ross believes me now, too,' she murmured, blowing her nose on a tissue from her bag. 'We've tried to get back together and it isn't working.' She gave an exasperated sigh. 'His place is here with you and the family, so I've decided I should be the one to go.'

'Does he know this?' Thomas

demanded, returning to his chair.

'I told him I was coming here to say goodbye to you.'

'Didn't he try to stop you?' His voice had lost none of its old power.

'No. He had other things to see to.' Her eyes pleaded with his. 'I'm sorry, Thomas, for everything.'

'You have nothing to be sorry for. Please stay — you have a job you enjoy and that you're good at.'

'I did have,' she corrected him. 'We came to a mutual decision that my services were no longer required.'

'We'll see about that! In a month, I should be able to work part time and I want you there as my assistant.'

'I'm sure my replacement will be quite capable.'

'I'm not letting you go that easily!' he warned her.

'Please,' Emma begged. 'Don't make things harder than they already are.'

'Where will you go?'

She shrugged her shoulders.

'I promise I'll contact you when I get

to wherever I decide. I've got my car so I might take off and travel round a bit.'

'You have to stay for the grand opening of the complex,' he insisted. 'It's all your work.'

She shook her head.

'I don't think it's a good idea,' she declared, holding his stare. Taking a deep breath to summon up the courage she needed, she said, 'I promised Ross I'd never tell you but I feel it's time I broke that promise, for the sake of our friendship — yours and mine, that is. Thomas, he only asked me to marry him because of his loyalty to you. He did what he thought was the right thing.'

'I'm sorry, Emma, I'm not sure I know what you're talking about,' Thomas drawled, appearing totally bewildered.

'He didn't want you to look foolish so he asked me before you did,' she blurted out. 'I know it was wrong but I went along with his plan. It was stupid to think it would work and it hasn't!'

'Please! Slow down!' he said, gesturing with his hand but she leaped up from her chair.

'I've said too much already. I don't want you two to fight again on my account. Please promise me you won't say anything,' she begged, fresh tears beginning to stream down her face. 'And please promise you'll come and visit.'

'On one condition, Emma,' he countered sternly. 'That you accompany me to the opening.'

'I can't!'

'Forget Ross, forget everyone — I want you there with me. If anyone deserves to be there it's you.' He stood up, his head held high. 'And I'll tell that son of mine, if he's going to cause a scene, I'll cancel the whole thing.'

'You can't do that!' she insisted.

'Watch me,' he replied, his eyes twinkling with mischief. 'I'll expect you there at seven o'clock. I'll be waiting at the door for you. If you don't turn up or he doesn't mind his manners then I'll call it off — however late in the day it is.'

'OK.' She sighed. 'I'm leaving town this afternoon so you won't be able to contact me. But I'll do my best to be there.'

'And please wear his necklace. I'd like to see it for one last time.'

Eventually she tore herself from his paternal embrace, trying to control herself but not succceeding. Flying through the house to her car, she quickly started it up before she had a change of heart or Ross remembered where she was going. Why was she fooling herself? He didn't care — he never had!

Driving down the main street in town, she couldn't help but look out for his red car. Marshall said he'd seen them together here and she guessed Lindy had taken a room at one of the guest houses until they found some-where more permanent.

Calling the airline when she returned

to her flat, she reserved a seat on the next flight down to Savannah. She had to put miles between her and Ross if she was going to be ready to face him and Lindy at the opening.

★   ★   ★

On arriving in Savannah, she caught a taxi to the centre of town and checked into a large hotel near the historic waterfront.

Turning on the television as she unpacked her small case, she half-listened to the voices of the newscasters.

'And now over to you, Bob, for an update,' the woman remarked. Emma hung up the dress she'd brought along to wear for dinner tonight. Not that she was hungry, but her appetite might return when her shock dwindled.

'As you can see from our satellite pictures,' the newscaster declared seriously, 'this is where the trouble lies in the Atlantic. These are the latest we've received from the Hurricane Centre in Miami.'

Emma returned to the bed and found her toiletries. Taking them to her ensuite bathroom, he was still chatting when she got back. The newscaster's map caught her eye. It was of the south-eastern States of America.

'At present, the storm is gathering speed though it's not yet at hurricane force. It's being predicted to hit the Florida coast in the early hours of Friday morning.'

Now spellbound, Emma shivered. She detested the hurricane season although it had been eight years since South Carolina had been badly hit. She watched the storm's path as predicted on the screen by the sophisticated computers and sighed with relief it wasn't hitting their coast.

Going out with her pad and box of charcoals, Emma headed for the river. It was early evening and the sky was still cloudless as she settled herself on a bench, ready to lose herself in her sketching.

★   ★   ★

The next morning, although she hadn't slept well in the strange bed, she forced herself to get up and by two o'clock, she had sketched some quaint, restored eighteenth-century houses and views in some of the seventeen parks laid out when the city was settled. Going to an estate agent's office, she picked up some brochures on houses to buy and rent.

The money she'd got from selling her father's house in London was still untouched in her bank account. She could afford a small two-bedroomed place so that it was big enough to welcome guests.

Suddenly all her troubles welled up again and she was confronted by Ross's vision. She loved him so much! She rubbed her eyes wishing she could forget him. While she had unfinished business in Beaufort, she couldn't hope to think of the future. She made the decision there and then to go back.

Packing again, she waited at the airport for two and a half hours for the tiny plane to arrive. That was the trouble with Beaufort airport — its runway couldn't take larger planes. As they took off, she gripped the arm of her seat and contented herself with the thought that she was on her way home.

Taking a short cut through the town of Beaufort to her flat, she cursed when her car's engine started to splutter. Gazing down at the fuel gauge, she swore more vehemently, now at herself for not checking her petrol before she left yesterday. She managed to get her car into the kerb before it gave a final lurch.

Sighing, she took her bags from the car, locked up, then strode towards her flat. She knew Marshall lived in this area and that he'd want to help her, but she felt she couldn't face anyone tonight. Maybe in the morning she'd call him.

Unpacking, Emma decided that, the following day, she'd retrieve the necklace from the bank. She wasn't sure if she could keep her promise to Thomas, but she was certain whether she wore it or not, she was going to return it. It belonged in the Hamilton family — of which she wouldn't be a member for much longer.

After getting changed for bed, she made some warm milk and headed for her bedroom. She also took a sleeping tablet to ensure a good night's rest.

She turned on the portable television at the end of her bed and watched the last part of a film, propped up on her pillows. She tried to write a note to go with her necklace that she would be dropping off with Charles the next day.

Tearing the sheet off the pad, she screwed it up and threw it to the floor to join the other discarded ones. She was beginning to feel pleasantly drowsy as she began another letter. Her head was heavier but it snapped up when she heard the film's finale music.

Rubbing her sore neck muscles, she settled down under her covers, not caring about the pad falling on to the carpet nor of the excited voice coming from the small screen. Sleep. She needed sleep. With a limp hand, she waved the control, trying to turn off the TV. As she plummeted into a deep sleep, the emergency weather bulletin faded to nothing.

* * *

'Emma! Emma!'

She was pushing Ross away from her. Someone was banging. Why wouldn't they leave her alone?

There was a loud crash and she stirred. For a moment her eyes flickered but the room was black. Fighting to get out of this dream which was becoming frightening, she tried to wake herself up.

'Emma! Are you in there?'

Her eyelids were lead-heavy and when she managed to open them, it made no difference — it was pitch black. And it was deathly quiet. Suddenly there came another crash and this time she heard wood splintering.

'Emma? Are you there? Answer me!'

'Ross?' she cried weakly, trying to pull herself up on her pillows.

'Emma?' There was a flicker of light from the lounge.

'I'm in here!' She heard her bedroom door creak when it was opened fully and she winced as she was dazzled by the brilliant beam.

'Thank God!' Ross proclaimed, putting his torch on the bed and throwing his arms around her. 'Come on, we have to get out of here.'

'Why? What?' Her head was so muzzy.

Ross directed the beam around her room. 'Put on some warm clothes. We're gonna have to get out of here, maybe for several days. You must have been in some deep sleep — I've been trying to wake you for ages.'

'Everything caught up with me — I was exhausted.' Emma felt like crying with fatigue. 'And I took something to help me sleep.'

'No wonder you missed the warnings. Wait there while I get you some clothes.'

In awe she watched him, lit by the torch's glow in the dark while he went through her chest of drawers and dragged out some items.

'Put these on!' he ordered, throwing her jeans to her. 'Hurry, Emma — we don't have much time.'

Opening her wardrobe, he began to make another search so she pulled her jeans on over her nightclothes, but the more she hurried, the more she fumbled.

'Do you have a flashlight?'

'In the kitchen, under the sink,' she said, struggling with the buttons on her jeans. He threw one of her jogging sweaters, a raincoat and a pair of trainers on to the bed.

'Here, use this one,' he told her pressing her torch in her hand moments later. 'I've got things to do.'

Although she did as she was ordered, she couldn't understand why he was here at the apartment or what was going on. He was making quite a noise around the place and she was just making her first tentative steps when he rushed back in. The beam of light was going around the room as he hurried and unplugged her television and lamps.

'We have to get down to the car, Emma.'

She cried out as she tripped over something and his arm went around her waist.

'Come on, I'll help you get to the front door.'

'I've hurt my foot, Ross, I'm not sure if I can.'

The tears stared to run down her cheeks — what on earth was going on?

In the light from their torches, she noticed her front door was broken.

'What have you done?' she cried, seeing the busted panel.

'I had to get in to see if you were here!'

They were at the top of the stairs but instead of helping her to the ground floor, Ross led her aside.

'Wait here and don't move!' He hurried back into the flat, returning a minute later with her quilt folded across the top of a cardboard box. 'Hold this torch for me while I go to the car.'

Emma's heart was thumping wildly, not knowing what was going on but realising this wasn't the moment to challenge Ross's orders.

'Ross, what's going on?'

He turned to face her.

'Listen to me, Em. We've got to get to the storm shelter at my father's house. There's a huge storm brewing and it's going to get worse. On the count of three, we're gonna have to make a run for it. Can you do it?'

'I'll try.' Her brain was now less foggy, but her legs felt very heavy.

The darkness and the sound of the wind whistling around the eaves was very spooky and goose pimples erupted on her skin.

'Ready?' Ross squeezed her tenderly. She nodded and braced herself. Her pulse thudded loudly in her head as he held the front door open with his free hand. 'One, two, three.'

Pushing Emma through the door first, he quickly gripped her across the shoulders and forced her to run with him. A gust of wind buffeted them as they cleared the corner of the house.

'Nearly there,' Ross shouted over the noise.

'Ow!' Her body jerked as her foot slid along the wet leaves brought down from a nearby tree.

Ross caught her and cursed under his breath. Steeling himself, in a sudden movement she was up in his arms and they were covering the last ten yards to the car. Ross let her inside and ran off into the darkness.

The rain was heavier and through the

windows she couldn't see him. In a breathless panic she watched for his figure outside and was relieved when he reappeared.

His door opened and he threw himself into his seat, slamming the door after him.

'Where did you go?' she asked as his engine started the first time of trying, its throaty exhaust growling.

'You left your keys inside. I locked the main front door to guard against looters. If there's anything left after tonight, I'll gladly have your door fixed.'

'Ross,' she pleaded.

'Let me concentrate,' he retorted but smiled across at her.

The wind was gusting stronger and Emma's fingers gripped the edge of her leather seat as they were buffeted across the road. Although it probably only took several minutes to drive there, she felt like it was a good deal longer.

'We're gonna have to get down to the basement,' Ross told her. 'We'll be safe there. I'll carry the box if you can take the quilt. Do you know where the side entrance is?'

She knew the layout of the property well but had always wondered where the short flight of stairs led down to. She nodded.

'Here's the key,' he said, pressing it into her palm. 'You'll have to go alone. I'll lock the car and follow you.'

Taking the folded quilt which she'd been wrapped up in less than an hour ago, Emma leaped out of the car — and ran as fast as she could down the side path. The rain was teeming down and she had to wipe her face to clear away the droplets to see properly.

Soon she had the door unlocked and took refuge in the darkened room. Locating her torch, she quickly turned it on and found a light switch on the bare wall. She flicked it and when nothing happened she knew the electricity must be off all over town.

Directing the torchlight around, she noted there were bulky items stored in here covered with plastic. She shivered.

Her raincoat was drenched but she didn't want to take it off otherwise she'd feel colder. A noise behind startled her.

Her heart was thudding as her light caught Ross bending to put the box from her apartment on the floor.

'What's happening?' she begged as she caught his breath loudly.

'The town has been evacuated because of the storms,' he puffed. 'There's a kerosene lamp over here for emergencies. We'll have to find it.'

Following him to the corner, Emma held both torches so Ross could sort through the boxes unencumbered. She saw one contained canned food and sealed canisters of water.

Soon Ross found the lamp and after setting it up, he lit it with a match and the flame illuminated the room with a reassuring glow.

'We'd better think about drying off these clothes if we don't want a chill,' he said removing his leather jacket and giving it a shake.

'So what's been going on?' Emma asked taking off her coat.

'There's a bad storm heading this way. Evacuation began a few hours ago. I'm surprised you didn't hear the warnings.'

'I heard of one yesterday on the television when I was in Savannah. They said it was heading for Florida though,' Emma said gazing up at him, drying her dripping hair with a towel from her box.

'It changed direction at sea and has ravaged the Georgia coastline. We're not in its direct path but there could be a lot of local damage.'

'Where's Thomas?'

'He's fine — safe with the others in the evacuation centre. We'd tried to contact you yesterday morning and your landlady said that you'd gone away. Your car wasn't in the driveway tonight so we assumed you weren't in.

'It wasn't until we met up with Marshall a short while ago that we learned he'd seen your car on the way to the centre. He wanted to know why you weren't with us.'

'I knew my personal number plate was a good idea.' She smiled.

Suddenly Ross let out a yell and rubbed his shoulder.

'What's the matter?' Emma asked in concern.

'I must have hurt myself when I broke your door — I had to put my shoulder to it and I think I've pulled something. Come on, let's get some chairs organised. We could have a long wait ahead of us.'

Without an argument, she helped him as they unwrapped the plastic sheet from what she now saw was an old settee. She tried to take much of the strain as they righted it.

'There's a mattress here, too, but we can find that in a minute.' Ross sighed as he collapsed into the dusty cushions, grimacing.

'Let me look at your arm,' Emma insisted standing over him.

'I put some pain-killers in the box.

Can you get them?'

She brought back the small container and the unopened carton of orange juice he'd taken from her fridge. Giving them to him, she found a bottle of water and one of their discarded towels.

'Could you take your shirt off?' she ordered him and painfully he unbuttoned it and slowly pulled it off.

When he'd done it and he was naked from the waist up, she could see the bad bruising showing through his deep tan. Crouching beside him, she started bathing his wound in the cool water.

'You're lucky there aren't any cuts.'

'I don't feel lucky.'

'Stop being a baby!' She smiled, hiding her worry. Her first-aid training told her one of his bones was at a peculiar angle. It was either dislocated or broken and he needed professional care.

'Just relax, Ross,' she said soothingly.

'That's not going to be easy while you're around.' The old twinkle was back in his green eyes.

Immediately Emma felt uncomfortable and got to her feet. 'I'm very grateful you helped me, Ross, but it doesn't change anything. Not when Lindy's waiting back at the centre for you,' she snapped angrily.

He tried to get to his feet but stopped as his face showed pain.

'Emma, honey, she's a private investigator.'

'Sure. And you happen to share the same flat!'

'Her fiancé works at the studios — she's living with him. I'm their tenant.'

'Then what was all that business at the office?'

'She's come here to find our thief.'

'So she hasn't taken my job?'

'No, of course not and if you'd stayed at Pop's longer I would have told you. As usual, you just did your own thing.' Turning the towelling so a colder part gave him relief, he sighed again. 'When I got there, Pop had worked himself into a state.'

'I'm sorry — I wasn't thinking very

clearly but I thought I'd explained everything to him.'

Ross shook his head slowly.

'He wanted me to fill him in on a few details. Damn it, Emma, why did you have to tell him?'

'I can't remember exactly what I did say.'

'He mentioned I'd married you out of loyalty to him. When will you realise I married you because I wanted to?'

'To help me, I know,' she countered, recalling his father's words that because of his previous experience he wouldn't marry for love.

He collapsed back on to the cushions, trying not to damage his shoulder any more. He couldn't hide the pain from his face.

'I married you to stop you from being deported but that was because I couldn't bear to lose you, Emma. Were you so blinded by my father's affection and him wanting so much to look after you that you couldn't see how much I loved you, really loved you?'

10

'What are you talking about, Ross?' she cried, her mouth dropping open in astonishment.

His eyes met hers as she stood rooted to the spot.

'I'd believed I'd never fall in love again — and certainly not at first sight!'

Crouching beside him, she held the water-soaked towel over his bruises, their faces close now.

'So I made up a few details,' he drawled, 'but I figured it was worth it. If you really knew what my intentions were, you'd have run a mile. I know I used your feelings of loyalty towards my father to my own advantage, but I could see you didn't want to go back to England. In that way, we were both satisfied.'

'But you never showed me any sign of how you felt. In fact, the longer we were together, the colder you became towards me,' she replied.

'That had a lot to do with my fiancée, Deanna,' he said with a slight tremor in his voice. 'I've never told you about her.'

'Thomas told me a bit the other afternoon.'

'I was there when it happened. She died in my arms.'

'Oh, Ross, I'm so sorry.'

'It had a huge impact on me. I was told it was the equipment used during the stunt which was faulty — there was a defect in it which was only detected during the forensic tests. No human eye could have noticed it.

'It didn't matter to me — I still held myself responsible for Deanna's death. I was just getting over it, when you arrived on the scene. I can remember that evening I walked in and you were sitting in the parlour with Pop.

'You looked so vulnerable sitting there,' he murmured, 'and so beautiful. It was your blue eyes that I noticed first but I decided I wasn't going to make any moves. I knew if I did, I'd probably scare you away. You seemed so delicate and naïve.'

'I don't think I was naïve,' she contested. 'I'd had boyfriends in England. But I admit I was in awe of your family then. When Thomas came over and invited me to stay in his home, I thought it was going to be a regular house.

'He didn't act in a flashy manner and when he'd mentioned the family business casually, I presumed it was a small concern, not one of the major real estate and development companies in the area.'

'That sounds like Pop — always the master of understatement.'

'I could hardly believe it when we pulled up outside this place and I saw how big it was. And to finish it off, a butler opened the door!'

Ross laughed and nodded.

'I felt totally out of my depth, Ross. We'd only been in about half an hour when you arrived.'

'That explains why you looked so startled.' He chuckled.

Emma knew the reason for that was seeing Ross for the first time — she'd never seen such an attractive man before.

'Your hand was trembling when I took it in mine. It seemed so small and delicate.' Holding it, he'd raised it to his lips and kissed it lightly. Now, he reached over and repeated his action, stirring that old sensation within her.

'You must be getting cold,' she remarked, deliberately tearing her hand from his grasp. 'I'll find something for you to put around yourself.'

'You've been wasted at the company. You'd make an excellent nurse,' he proclaimed as she found a stack of blankets in another box.

'It's a bit old but it'll do,' Emma said, coming back and sliding a blanket over his shoulders.

'I thought breaking that door would have been easier than the stunts I do but as it turned out . . . '

'The door was for real, Ross. Generally the stunts aren't,' she reminded him. 'You risked a lot for me tonight so once again I'm in your debt. I wish there was something I could do for you.'

'Stay in Beaufort. I realise now you know why I fooled you, you're more likely to move away, but I want you to stay. If not for me, for my father. I'd much rather be able to see you every day than lose you again and I'll promise to keep my jealousy on a tight rein.'

'Jealousy?'

'Why do you think I got so mad with you? You'd married me, but you were more interested in my father's well-being, always worrying about how he was! That really crushed me. And that's why I left. But believe me, a day didn't pass in Florida when I didn't think of you, honey. Hey, what's up?'

Tears of joy were falling from Emma's eyes.

'Please, hold me, Ross.' She sniffed.

'We're going to be safe,' he reassured her when she cuddled into his uninjured arm and he encompassed her body and hugged her to him. 'I'm sure the hurricane won't come near here.'

'You never told me it was a hurricane!' she cried. 'You said it was a bad storm — '

Ross's mouth came down on her lips and cut off her flow of words. As their kiss deepened in intensity, they clung to each other both knowing they should never have been apart. The love was impossible to deny.

Ross gave a moan as, with some effort, he pulled his head away from hers.

'Emma, we have to stop this.'

She stared at him with a puzzled expression.

'You're so vulnerable just now and I don't want you to think I'm taking advantage of the situation.' Swinging himself around, he got up. 'There should be some cans of drink in one of these boxes.'

'I can get them,' she told him.

'I'm not a complete invalid.' He glanced over his shoulder and smiled. 'And I need something to take my mind off you for the time being.'

Emma smiled at his honesty.

'Ross, you've been truthful with me but I don't think you're going to be amused when I tell you something.' She took a sip of drink to moisten her suddenly dry mouth. 'I've always loved Thomas as a father and never wanted to leave him. He was always so kind towards me.'

She watched his expression turn to one of astonishment.

'There was one evening when I found a lipstick mark on your shirt, do you remember? I felt humiliated and I lashed out at you. I'd have said anything at that moment rather than let you know how much I was hurting inside.' Her hand went to her heart, her mouth twisting as she recalled the heartache.

'I was your wife yet you didn't want

me. You tossed me aside for a mistress. I felt self-pity, hatred, jealousy. My self confidence hit rock bottom.'

'Did you say jealousy?' Ross demanded furiously.

'Yes!' she cried. 'You had always accused me of wanting to stay in the States because of your father and it was easier to let you believe it than tell you the truth that it was because I was in love with you!'

'You mean the last two and a half years have been for nothing?' he thundered, the intensity bringing her close to tears. 'I've been in exile in Florida, living in abject misery for nothing?' He raked his fingers through his hair. 'And I thought you were a terrible liar! Emma, you really did a job on me!'

'Then if you really did love me, how did you get lipstick on your collar?' she asked, her voice rising. It wasn't all her fault. 'You were missing from the house so often it was becoming obvious you were seeing someone else. Finding that

185

mark confirmed my suspicions.' She glowered at him. 'You didn't even try to come up with an excuse!'

'If it hadn't gone so far, I'd have told you the truth — I was having a house built for us up the coast. I was spending a lot of time with the architect and builders at the site. It's right on the beach and because it was a fine day, I decided to go for a swim.

'One of the young workmen had left his shirt back in the truck so I lent him mine as his shoulders were starting to burn. When he gave it back to me later, it was after his girlfriend had turned up, with his lunch apparently. But lunch had obviously gone by the wayside.'

'But you were so cold towards me when we first met and again a month or so before we broke up,' she protested.

'I admit to begin with I was alarmed by the strong feelings I had towards you. I'd already lost Deanna and I was being torn apart. I refused to admit to myself I'd fallen for you and I fought it for as long as I could. In the first few months of our marriage, we had some great times and I felt we were getting closer.'

'I remember,' she mused aloud.

'That day with Joshua on the beach, I felt there was a glimmer of hope when you returned my kiss with obvious feeling.'

Smiling, she blushed.

'I already owned the plot of land so the next week, I got things moving. Whenever I came home, you'd be chatting to Pop and I admit I became jealous that you were more at ease in his company than mine.'

'I was scared to be alone with you in case you realised I loved you. It was supposed to be a marriage of convenience.'

'Marriage of contrivance, you mean,' he said as he reached for her hand. 'I contrived the plan to build a home for us and get you to live with me and I had to get you to agree before it was too late. But it all went so wrong, didn't it? We have been such fools.

Come here,' he drawled, tugging her towards him and he kissed her passionately.

'Does that mean our divorce is off now?' she murmured when she was allowed to pull away to catch her breath.

'What do you think?' He chuckled deeply and she felt it echo around his body close to hers.

'Shouldn't we tune into my radio you brought along, to find out what's happening?'

'We're quite safe in here and my family are safe at the Centre.' He drew her towards him and beamed at her. 'We've got plenty of time later to discover what the storm has done. This might not be the most romantic spot in the world, but right now, Mrs Hamilton, I think we should be more worried about repairing the damage our love has suffered. Don't you?'

★   ★   ★

The full-length sapphire satin gown was heavy but Emma strolled with ease, taking her husband's uninjured arm as they entered the large entrance hall of the complex.

She smiled, noting the decorations for the grand opening were as she'd ordered. It had been a week since the storm and as there had been little damage to the complex, their opening had only been delayed by a couple of days.

Thomas, immaculately dressed in a tuxedo and looking very happy, was the first to greet them.

'You made it back in time. How was Florida?' She blushed as Thomas kissed her cheek.

'We didn't get everything sorted out but we managed to accomplish a fair amount,' Ross replied, smiling. 'When I can coax my wife away from her work for a longer period of time, we'll be having a proper honeymoon.'

Ross was joking; actually, they had both been toiling at the office for hours to sort out the damage left by their thieving employee and ensuring it couldn't happen again as easily. Only the last three days had been spent in Florida, arranging his move back to South Carolina.

'Has Lindy arrived yet?' Emma asked and Thomas nodded.

'She's through there.' His eyes dipped to her bare shoulders. In pride of place, her necklace was glittering under the lights. 'It's beautiful.'

Standing on tiptoe, Emma kissed Ross's cheek.

'Isn't it — I couldn't have asked for a more perfect gift.'

'And I couldn't have asked for a more perfect wife,' Ross replied with a smile.

Thomas took Emma's other arm and the three of them together strolled into the large room which would serve as the community's lounge and restaurant from the following day. She felt ecstatic to see her plans for its decor had come to fruition. Making their way slowly through the gathering, greeting old friends and also ones she'd sold the surrounding bungalows to, they eventually reached the bar.

Lindy looked gorgeous in her red gown although the first thing which Emma noticed was the ring that the brunette was sporting on her second finger.

'Can I have a few words?' Emma whispered, indicating a spot away from their group.

Lindy joined her.

'You don't have to say anything.'

'I do,' Emma insisted. 'I was so rude to you and you weren't in Orlando so I could apologise.'

Holding up her hand, Lindy beamed.

'We went to see my parents and make it official. Graeme had only proposed the day before you got there. Ross took us out to celebrate and I was still suffering the after-effects when you turned up at our apartment.'

'I also want to say thanks for your

detective work. You did a great job finding out who did it.'

'With a lot of help from you.' Lindy squeezed Emma's arm. 'You were marvellous as the aggrieved wife. The way you looked at me in Orlando I wondered then if Ross wasn't mistaken. In confidence, he told us about his scam and that he had himself to blame for it backfiring.

'He called me to help because he knew I'd been on a similar case recently. When you stormed into his office and I saw your expression, I knew I could play on it and get the results I was looking for.'

'At least you ignored my tantrum and did what you were there to do!'

'I knew you were both being stubborn and you'd get it together when it was all over.'

'But why did Jacqui do it? Did she ever say?'

'She mumbled something about getting her own back,' Lindy remarked casually.

'For what? Why did she want to set me up?'

'Because she was jealous of you,' Lindy replied, sighing.

Lindy had been called as a witness by the police and had been there with Ross when the woman was arrested. Ross had filled Emma in with the barest of details adding it was the future that mattered.

Lindy regarded her and seemed to assess that Emma wasn't going to let the matter end yet.

'When Thomas promoted you to his personal assistant a few months ago, Jacqui felt the job was rightfully hers. I think, also, she noticed how friendly you were with him.'

'She joined after Ross had left me.'

'And as you called yourself Taylor, she didn't suspect he was your father-in-law. Perhaps she saw Thomas as a good prospect, him being a wealthy widower — I don't know, I'm just guessing. With you out of the way, she was next in line for your job.'

'She didn't expect you to turn up as my replacement so soon.'

'And fortunately that's when she made her first mistake. She was so annoyed, she didn't wait for the cheque to be sent to the bogus address. I saw her going through the stack and take it. By the time I alerted Ross, she was already heading off, supposedly for her lunch break.'

'But how did she pull it off?' Emma implored. 'The cheque was made out to the firm it should have gone to.'

'Are you going to be hiding here in a corner all night, honey?' Ross asked as he slid his arm around her satin-clad waist and she trembled under his touch.

'Just a moment,' she pleaded with her voice and eyes.

'Jacqui set up a dummy company which had the same initials as the firm you regularly sent cheques to. As their full name wasn't given on the cheques, just the initials, she paid them into her own account. When the owner of the real firm was confronted, he said a woman used to deliver the payments in cash.

'He knew Thomas had some strange business ideas and accepted it was his peculiar way of doing things. He didn't say anything because he was being paid promptly. At police headquarters, he identified Jacqui as the woman who usually made the deliveries.'

'Usually?' Emma said in disbelief. 'There was more than one?'

Ross tried to lead her away but she resisted.

'Kind of,' Ross cut in. 'She used you as a scapegoat. Did you go to the firm's site office a week or two ago?'

'Yes. I had to finalise something.' She hit her brow with her hand. 'She asked me if I could deliver their invoice because she was busy with the project work I'd delegated to her!'

'Don't take it personally, Emma. She was covering herself in every way she could,' Lindy said as they returned to the others who had been joined in their absence by members of their staff.

Marshall withdrew his arm from his new girlfriend at his side and stepped forward to give Emma a warm hug.

'I'm pleased everything's turned out for you. And thanks for inviting us to the ceremony. We're absolutely delighted.'

'Ceremony? What ceremony?' Emma asked, looking at the happy faces.

Laughing, Ross caught her arm and drew her to one side.

'It was supposed to be a surprise.' His eyes twinkled mischievously. 'We're getting married next week — on our anniversary.'

'We're already married, silly!' she chortled, pointing to her wedding ring now back in its rightful place on her left hand.

'No, I mean for real. I thought we should renew our vows in church in front of our friends and family. We may have been hiding our love the first time around, but now everyone will see how happy I am to have you as my wife. You included, Em.'

As his lips came down to touch hers, she knew they'd weathered their stormy passage and from now on, it would be plain-sailing with her very loyal, loving husband at her side.

THE END

We do hope that you have enjoyed reading this large print book.

Did you know that all of our titles are available for purchase?

We publish a wide range of high quality large print books including:
Romances, Mysteries, Classics
General Fiction
Non Fiction and Westerns

Special interest titles available in large print are:
The Little Oxford Dictionary
Music Book, Song Book
Hymn Book, Service Book

Also available from us courtesy of Oxford University Press:
Young Readers' Dictionary
(large print edition)
Young Readers' Thesaurus
(large print edition)

For further information or a free brochure, please contact us at:
Ulverscroft Large Print Books Ltd.,
The Green, Bradgate Road, Anstey,
Leicester, LE7 7FU, England.
Tel: (00 44) **0116 236 4325**
Fax: (00 44) **0116 234 0205**

TOO MANY LOVES

Juliet Gray

Justin Caldwell, a famous personality of stage and screen, was blessed with good looks and charm that few women could resist. Stacy was a newcomer to England and she was not impressed by the handsome stranger; she thought him arrogant, ill-mannered and detestable. By the time that Justin desired to begin again on a new footing it was much too late to redeem himself in her eyes, for there had been too many loves in his life.

MYSTERY AT MELBECK

Gillian Kaye

Meg Bowering goes to Melbeck House in the Yorkshire Dales to nurse the rich, elderly Mrs Peacock. She likes her patient and is immediately attracted to Mrs Peacock's nephew and heir, Geoffrey, who farms nearby. But Geoffrey is a gambling man and Meg could never have foreseen the dreadful chain of events which follow. Throughout her ordeal, she is helped by the local vicar, Andrew Sheratt, and she soon discovers where her heart really lies.

HEART UNDER SIEGE

Joy St Clair

Gemma had no interest in men — which was how she had acquired the job of companion/secretary to Mrs Prescott in Kentucky. The old lady had stipulated that she wanted someone who would not want to rush off and get married. But why was the infuriating Shade Lambert so sceptical about it? Gemma was determined to prove to him that she meant what she said about remaining single — but all she proved was that she was far from immune to his devastating attraction!